MURDER
in
TINSEL TOWN

MURDER

_in_

TINSEL TOWN

Max Nightingale

Harper
North

HarperNorth
Windmill Green
24 Mount Street
Manchester M2 3NX

A division of
HarperCollins*Publishers*
1 London Bridge Street
London SE1 9GF

www.harpercollins.co.uk

HarperCollins*Publishers*
Macken House, 39/40 Mayor Street Upper
Dublin 1, D01 C9W8, Ireland

First published by HarperNorth in 2024

24 25 26 27 28 LBC 5 4 3 2 1

A catalogue record for this book
is available from the British Library

HB ISBN: 978-0-00-872630-0
TPB ISBN: 978-0-00-874655-1

Printed and bound in the United States.

FOR AM, H AND B – HERE'S LOOKING
AT YOU, KIDS

CHAPTER ONE

B lanche Aikerman stares blankly at the last meal she's ever going to eat. There's not much to it, just a simple salad. A bottle of champagne – Dom Perignon, naturally – is sitting cooling in an ice bucket beside the table. She's not hungry. Not thirsty. She's got no appetite at all.

This was supposed to be a happy weekend, a chance to celebrate. She is, after all, the most famous woman in the world. What was it *Variety* said about her? 'An actor of generational talent and looks to die for.' The thought makes her cringe. Yes, she may be Hollywood's flavour of the month, but it's lonely at the top.

She gets up from the edge of the bed. Her penthouse suite at the top of the Royale Premiere overlooks Los Angeles. Above the city's hazy cloud of smog and fumes, on the famous hills *that* sign looks down. Blanche stares at it. 'Hollywood' in huge, crumbling, tattered letters stares back, like a giant eye, silently laughing at her. Blanche had read *The Great Gatsby* when she was a teenager – one of the few fond memories of her time growing up. Giant eyes were always there, looking down on the characters, it had creeped her out. Now here she was, in Tinseltown, being watched by her own Doctor T. J. Eckleburg. Seeing it in disrepair, she knows all too well how it feels. Being famous, being a star, comes at a price.

'Here's looking at you, kid,' she says with a mocking laugh.

A knock at the door distracts her. She turns away from the balcony door and walks through the suite. The place is a mess, she's not bothered to clean and asked not to be disturbed. She can do what she likes – she's Blanche Aikerman, after all.

The knocking continues, getting louder and more frantic. She pulls the door open, ready to scream at whatever unsuspecting fool has dared interrupt her dinner.

'Where the hell have you been?'

It's Peter von Hiltz, director extraordinaire, the man who's brought all of this on Blanche over the last five, stellar, years.

'Everyone is waiting for you, you should have been downstairs thirty minutes ago,' he says, storming into the suite.

'I'm trying to have dinner,' says Blanche, running a hand through her long dark hair. 'Why don't you come in, Peter, take a load off, stay a while.'

The director stops in the middle of the suite and looks at the mess. He tuts loudly.

'I see you're enjoying the all-expenses-paid hospitality,' he says, kicking an empty champagne bottle with his over-polished riding boot. 'Nice to see the studio is getting its money's worth.'

'If you're here to tell me how bad a person I am, you're too late,' says Blanche. 'My mom already has that covered. She'll be here in a minute, maybe you two can make a team.'

'I'm here to make sure you're on time, Blanche. There's the small matter of you becoming the toast of the Hollywood glitterati. Remember?'

'How could I forget?' she says under her breath.

Peter hears her but he chooses to ignore her. He rounds and stares at her, his face getting redder with anger. He keeps his temper in check and reaches into his pocket. He pulls out an envelope and hands it to her.

'What's this, Peter, a Valentine's Card?' she asks with a smirk.

'It's a contract,' he says.

'For what?'

'For more money than either of us can count, Blanche,' he snaps. 'Thundersaga Pictures wants you and me on lifetime deals. Sign on the dotted line and we become theirs for life; any movie, any fee, you name it, sweetheart. This is what you've always wanted.'

'What *I've* always wanted; yeah right,' she snorts.

'Don't be a hero, Blanche, it doesn't suit you,' he says scornfully. 'Just sign the contract and we can argue about your self-loathing afterwards. Mr Ramsay is an impatient man, he doesn't give actors and directors a lot of time to make up their minds.'

Blanche looks at the envelope in Peter's hands. She lets him stew for a minute, his face so red it's turning purple. Money always does that to the director. She's known him for a long time, for as long as she's been in Hollywood. He has a reputation as a hitmaker but it's not about the art for Peter von Hiltz, no matter what he says to the press. He's in it for the money. And it gets his blood pressure going, has him fit to burst; stretched, like a balloon pumped with too much air. She snatches the envelope from him.

'I'll think about it,' she says, strolling confidently past him.

'You'll *think* about it?' he sneers.

'That's what I said, Peter.' She waves the envelope around in her hand. 'I'll think about it. I've got a busy schedule, as you know. I'll see about taking a look when I've got a couple of minutes.'

Peter is furious. He bunches his hands into fists, but he can't bring himself to say anything. He stops short of stomping his feet like a petulant child and instead marches to the door of the suite.

'Don't let that thing hit you on the way out, darling,' she calls back to him from the bedroom.

The director slams the door closed as hard as he can. When he's gone, Blanche sits back down on the edge of the bed and stares out of the balcony doors again at Los Angeles beyond.

Everything she ever wanted. The words go around and around in her head. Everything she ever wanted. If only that were true. Here she was, with more fame and money than anyone would ever know what to do with. She was no different to the people out there. She was just a country girl from the sticks who got lucky. Good looks, a little bit of talent and a dogged determination was what got her here, now, on top of the world. So why wasn't she happy?

Another knock at the door interrupts her daydream. She rolls her eyes.

'I'll read the contract when I'm ready, Peter,' she shouts.

The knocking continues. Blanche's malaise gives way to anger of her own. She throws the contract onto the bed and storms out of the bedroom. Cursing under her breath, she makes her way to the door of the penthouse and pulls it open. It's a decision she'll regret for the rest of her life and the final few minutes of it.

CHAPTER TWO

~~~~~~

Your phone rings. Your phone never stops ringing. It's one of the professional hazards of being a homicide detective in Los Angeles. For a city with over 200,000 people, they sure liked to try and keep the numbers down.

To make matters worse, it's the weekend of the big Golden Star Awards. All the celebrities are in town. And that usually makes things a hundred times worse for you. From crank calls to bomb threats, stalkers to gangsters, everyone wants a slice of the Tinseltown madness when the awards are being handed out. How you managed to get the weekend shift, you'll never know. But it means things are going to be busy – *real* busy.

You pick up the phone. At first there's no voice on the other end. You think the folks on the switchboard are having you on. It wouldn't be the first time. April Fools' day in this place is almost as mad as this weekend. But the line is live. You reiterate to whoever is on the other end that they're through to the LAPD and ask what they want.

Heavy breathing is the reply. You ask if everything is okay. No response. Whoever has called is nervous. You can hear the air catching in their throat. There's still nothing from them and you begin to think that it's nothing more than a prank.

Then they try to speak. It's quiet, indecipherable. You try to make out what they're saying but it's hard, they sound like they're far away from the phone.

'Trouble … hurt … not my fault … help… it's them … I'm sorry.'

Distant footsteps thud from somewhere. Then the line goes dead. You hang up the phone and make a note to have a word with those tricksters on the switchboard.

The squad room is busy, as usual. There are plenty of other detectives all running about shouting and bawling at each other. The holding cell at the front desk is full of perps, some innocent, some drunk, some guilty as hell. It's a noisy place and sometimes you wish you had a bit more peace and quiet, like Captain Barclay.

He's nowhere to be seen today, probably out golfing with the mayor and commissioner. Some guys have all the luck.

What was that person trying to say? They sounded sedate, like they'd taken something. Probably another one of the bums trying to waste police time. LA was home to every crank under the sun. And they all usually passed through the LAPD at some point.

Today's newspapers are sitting on your desk in front of you. To distract you from the hustle and bustle while the phone stays quiet, you pick up the *LA Times*. The front page is dominated by coverage of the Golden Star Awards. There's a huge picture of Blanche Aikerman. She's smiling, playing it pretty for the cameras at some red-carpet affair.

'Blanche knocks them out with her winning smile as star looks set to be crowned the Queen of Hollywood.'

She's an actress, a big-time star. For the last ten years you'd be hard pressed to find anyone on the planet who hadn't heard of Blanche Aikerman. From biblical epics to westerns and mobster movies, she's dazzled audiences from here to China. And she's attractive, too. Long, black hair that's darker than a raven's belly and a figure to die for – it's no wonder she's dubbed the 'Modern Cleopatra'. With a list of boyfriends as long as your arm, the press and the public can't get enough of her. She's one of the richest and most powerful women in the world.

The story talks about her being on the verge of winning big at the Goldies. Her turn as Boudica – already the highest grossing film of both 1957 and 1958 – is going to smash all kinds of records and she's finally going to get the recognition she deserves. It goes on to talk about what she'll be able to command in fees, all at the tender age of just twenty-seven. The world is at her feet, and everyone wants a little slice of Blanche Aikerman for themselves.

'Hey! You can't drink in here!' somebody shouts from the front desk.

'The hell I can't!' comes the angry reply.

A fight breaks out and distracts you from the paper. You put it down, but something is eating away at you. That damn phone call. *What was going on there?* It wasn't like the usual cranks, there was no punchline, no giggling from kids down the other end of the line. There wasn't even a threat you'd spend hours hunting out on a wild goose chase. Nothing. Just breathing and those broken words.

You decide to do a little digging, while you've still got the time. You call up the switchboard.

'Oh hi, hun, what can I do for ya.' It's Margot, one of the nicer, more competent operators. She listens to your request, then says, 'I didn't patch anyone through to you just then, but I can find out from one of the other gals where it came from. Gimme a sec, okay?'

You let Margot do her own investigation. While you wait, you sketch down what you remember the voice saying to you.

Trouble. Hurt. Not my fault. Help. It's them. I'm sorry.

The phone rings and you pick it up. It's Margot.

'Okay, you aren't going to believe this, hun,' she says. 'Looks like that call for you just came from the Royale Premiere hotel on Sunset Boulevard.'

A five-star haunt of all the rich and famous when they're in town. Not only that, but it's the venue for the Goldies tomorrow night.

'Yeah, seems that the call came through to us, but nobody was talking so we transferred it straight through to the squad room,' says Margot. 'And you were the unlucky stiff that got the mystery line. That's all I've got I'm afraid. Hope this helps.'

You thank Margot and hang up. You don't know how to describe it. Maybe it's just a hunch. Or police officer instinct. But you think there's something wrong, something that's not adding up. *A mystery call from a famous hotel? On the city's busiest weekend of the year?* You don't believe in coincidences, not in this line of work.

You grab your Mac, your hat, your gun and car keys to one of the department cruisers and head out of the chaos of the squad room.

CHAPTER THREE

———~~~———

The entranceway to the Royale Premiere is awash with people. Staff, guests and the world's press have gathered outside as final preparations for the glitzy awards ceremony are put in place. As you pull up to the front door, journalists and photographers all flock to the door.

You open the door and are blinded by the flashes of camera bulbs. A chorus of questions are volleyed your way as keen male and female journalists all vie for a scoop – starved of some celebrity gossip for five minutes. As you climb out of the car, you flash your LAPD badge and a collective groan travels through the throng.

'It's just the cops,' one says, disappointed.

'I thought it was somebody famous,' says another.

'No need to worry, nothing to see here,' somebody else comments.

You make your way into the hotel. Everywhere you look there are famous and semi-famous faces. Some are enjoying drinks at the bar, or lounging around the lobby. Other guests are sheepishly trying to sneak autographs while the staff vacuum, clean, tidy and build the last of the work ahead of tomorrow night's ceremony.

The reception desk is directly ahead. You walk over and ring the bell. A tall man with a bald head and prim little moustache greets you.

'Hello and welcome to the Royale Premiere. Are you checking in or dropping off?' he asks.

When you show him your badge, his friendliness immediately vanishes.

'Oh, the police,' he says with a sneer. 'My name is Mr Walter, I'm the manager of this establishment. What can I do to help you?'

You explain the phone call you received about thirty minutes ago. He seems perplexed.

'And you're sure it came from here?' he asks. 'That doesn't sound like the sort of thing that would happen at the Royale Premiere. Especially today or this weekend. Our guests are the crème de la crème of Hollywood. They're not some punk teenagers out looking to waste police time.'

It's clear that he's trying to save face. You remind him that you're a police officer and you have to take these kinds of things seriously. And that any and all cooperation with the LAPD is always greatly appreciated.

'Yes, of course,' he corrects himself. 'Well, I don't really know what to say. Whatever the guests do in their own rooms and suites is entirely up to them. As I'm sure you can appreciate, given our clientele, we hold confidentiality in very high regard here. The people who frequent our premises are among the most high-profile and famous in the land. You wouldn't want us listening in on their private conversations, would you? That would, after all, be a crime.'

Before you can press on, a man appears beside you. He barges you out of the way a little, arms flailing wildly.

'This is a disgrace. An absolute disgrace!' he shouts.

Mr Walter is immediately distracted by him. You vaguely recognise the man and rack your memory to place his face. Then you remember – Peter von Hiltz, the director. He's about the most infamous director in Hollywood, the papers and rumour mills abuzz with how he treats his stars on set. A perfectionist, he has more Goldies than he knows what to do with. He seems uncontrollably angry, like an agitated toddler.

'Where is Blanche? Where is my star?' he shouts at Walter.

'Mr von Hiltz, I—'

'*Herr* von Hiltz!' the director snaps.

'Yes, of course, Herr von Hiltz, I don't know where Miss Aikerman is, she hasn't been seen by myself or any of my staff since last night.'

'You're trying to tell me you've lost the most famous woman in the world?'

'No, yes, I mean …'

Walter looks at you for support. When he realises that's not going to happen, he tries to reason with the director.

'I can call up to her penthouse apartment, if you like, although the phone line seems to be engaged at the moment,' said Walter. 'But if it's important, I can send someone up.'

'Do it!' von Hiltz barks. 'And as soon as you've got her, let me know immediately. We have lines to rehearse, and I'm a busy, impatient man. You come straight to my suite as soon as you've found her. Got that?'

He gives you a dirty glare and then spins on his heels. Marching off through the lobby, you watch him until he's disappeared.

'I'm sorry about that, detective,' says Walter, looking exhausted. 'Herr von Hiltz is one of this hotel's most prestigious guests. We like to look after our stars here, as you can probably appreciate, can't you? Now, what was it I could help you with again?'

There's a commotion from behind the long reception desk. A young man appears at the far end, dressed like a waiter, his face ashen white.

'Mr Walter!' he shouts.

The other staff all clear out of the way as he runs towards the manager. Tripping, Walter has to catch him before he falls flat on his face.

'Carter, what the hell do you think you're doing?' asked Walter. 'Have you lost your mind? You can't shout like that in front of the guests.'

'No, sorry sir, it's just … it's just…'

'What is it? Out with it, boy!'

'She's dead, sir,' he says. 'Blanche Aikerman is dead. She's been murdered!'

CHAPTER FOUR

⌇

'She's dead? What do you mean she's dead? She can't be dead, she's the star of the show!'

Walter and Carter rush out from behind the desk and are walking quickly ahead of you now, down the uppermost corridor of the Royal Premiere. In the last few minutes things have gone from the mundane to the ridiculous. This was just a routine follow-up on a prank call. Now, it would seem, there's a murder on your hands. After making sure nobody else heard what Carter had said, Walter ushers you both into a back elevator that goes straight to the penthouse floor. The place is lavishly decorated and everything feels and looks expensive.

Up ahead are two double-doors. One has been left slightly ajar, a trolley full of food parked just beside it.

'I was delivering room service,' says Carter, out of breath and still pale. 'I've been doing it for the last two days since Miss Aikerman arrived. She barely eats anything, although she's very specific – half a grapefruit every afternoon at two, with a side order of champagne. Dom Perignon, naturally. I was bringing it up this afternoon when I saw that the door was open. I knocked, went inside and, well, you'll see.'

'Are you sure she's dead?' asks the manager.

'What?'

'Are you sure that she's dead? She might just be having a nap. You know what these celebrities are like, they're up to all hours at parties and galas. It's still early afternoon.'

'Just wait until you see,' says Carter.

'You haven't told anyone else have you, Carter?' asks Walter. 'Not another living soul knows about any of this?'

'No, sir,' he replies.

'This is absolutely the last thing we need,' says Walter. 'Not today, not when the awards are just a day away. This isn't what the hotel nor I, for that matter, needs.'

You reach the entrance to the penthouse. Walter knocks as Carter hangs around at the door, fumbling with the buttons on his waistcoat.

'Hello? Miss Aikerman? Are you there?' Walter asks.

The penthouse is dark. The curtains are drawn and there are no lights on. Walter flips a switch and the place illuminates. Everything seems in place. The furniture is put away, wardrobe doors closed, nothing out of place. It's as if nobody has ever set foot in the room at all.

You follow Walter, your hand not far from your gun, just in case. The main living room of the penthouse is just as pristine. There's nobody about, everything is as it seems. You spot what appears to be the way to the bedrooms and nod.

'Yes, okay,' says Walter. 'Maybe I should ... just stay here. In case anybody else comes in, that is.'

You agree and head over to the bedroom door yourself. A cool breeze is blowing through the open doorway. It carries with it the smell of perfume; sweet, like strawberries. With your hand still on your gun, you ease your way slowly into the huge bedroom.

The bed is directly ahead. A mighty four-poster with drapes around all sides. You notice that the door to the balcony is closed but there's still a breeze. It's not important just now. What *is* important is the pale, limp arm hanging over the side of the bed.

You look about the bedroom to make sure nobody is there. It's clear. Then, hurrying over to the bed, you pull back the drape, revealing the lifeless body of Blanche Aikerman.

Her face is slack, eyes open, with a sort of half-smile etched on her lips. A pool of dark blood has seeped into the bedding and it's clear, even from this angle, that her throat has been cut. The most famous woman in the world is staring back at you with lifeless, dead eyes. As far as murder victims go, she's about the best dressed one you've ever seen – a long, flowing dress covering the rest of the bed.

'Oh, my god!'

It's Walter, standing behind you. You didn't hear him come in. Either that or he's incredibly light on his feet.

'Oh, my god, it's true! She's dead. Blanche Aikerman is dead! In my hotel! Oh, my god. I have to tell Herr von Hiltz! I have to let him know!'

He runs out of the bedroom. You've got no choice but to follow him. The last thing you need is a mass panic on your hands. This place is now a crime scene. And it's your collar.

CHAPTER FIVE

———~~~———

Y ou knock on the door of the suite. Beside you is Mr Walter, the hotel manager. Carter, the waiter, is hovering around with you. His panic seems to have passed and he's acting a little cocky. He knows he holds valuable information, that only a few people in the whole world are privy to. For the first time in his life, he's part of the elite.

There's no answer from the door. Walter seems a little perturbed. He's nervous, too; sweaty, shifting from foot to foot.

'I'm sorry about this, detective,' says Walter. 'He instructed me to tell him as soon as we found Miss Aikerman. I can't believe she's dead, though. I mean, how *can* she be dead, she was larger than life.'

'And only twenty-seven, too,' says Carter.

'Yes, she was only twenty-seven. Just a child. It's such a tragedy. And awful timing, on the eve of these awards. Herr von Hiltz will know what to do.'

'Oh, yes,' says the waiter. 'He's been looking after us very well.'

Walter knocks impatiently on the suite door again.

'Herr von Hiltz,' he calls. 'It's Mr Walter, the hotel manager. We have some terrible news. The LAPD are here with me. It's about Miss Aikerman. We've found her, sir. You must come immediately.'

There's no answer from the other side of the door. Walter is starting to get anxious. He rubs his chin, looking between you, Carter and the door.

'I don't understand it,' he says to you.

Walter tries once more, this time thumping on the door of the hotel suite.

'Herr von Hiltz! It's Mr Walter. I have the police here for you, sir. You instructed us to fetch you as soon as we found Miss Aikerman … Herr von Hiltz?'

'Maybe he's in the john,' Carter sniggers.

'That's enough, Carter,' said Walter. 'I'm sorry officer, I don't really know what to say. This is most out of character from

Herr von Hiltz. He's a very precise, reliable guest of ours. I can't understand what's the matter.'

You look around the empty corridor of the hotel. You're starting to think something is going on here beyond the apparent murder of Blanche Aikerman. Being ushered away to von Hiltz's suite is very unusual behaviour, especially now that he's not answering the door.

What's going on here? Secrets and lies, that's nothing new for this town. But stopping a cop from doing their job, that's conspiracy.

There's a crime scene that has to be examined.
What do you do?

- You insist Mr Walter takes you back to the crime scene

  (turn to page 47)

- Ask Mr Walter to let you in von Hiltz's room? (turn to the next

  page 27)

- You ask Carter if he has any more information (turn to

  page 131)

'Open the room?' Walter asks. 'Are you sure? We pride ourselves on our discretion here at the Royale Premiere. I'm not sure this is a very good idea.'

'It's the cops, Mr Walter,' insists Carter. 'I think if they want you to open a door, you had better do it. Otherwise *you'll* end up in the slammer.'

Walter takes a brief moment to consider this. He adjusts the collar of his shirt and then fishes out his master key. He unlocks the door and pushes it open.

The strong smell of gasoline meets you all. Walter coughs and chokes as he holds a handkerchief to his mouth.

You press on, despite the smell. The suite is in complete disarray. Tables are turned over, drawers pulled from their shelves. Clothes, dirty plates and pages of script are strewn across the whole suite. The balcony door ahead of you is wide open, a gentle breeze making the cotton curtain flap a little. It does nothing to help the smell, which only gets stronger the further you move into the room.

'Herr von Hiltz!' Walter shouts. 'Are you here sir? Is everything alright?'

There's no answer. You look about the suite searching for answers but there's too much to take in. Then you spot the door to the en suite. It's slightly ajar and the sound of running water is drifting out. Carefully you make your way to the door.

'Herr von Hiltz?' Walter is still shouting.

You knock on the bathroom door. No response. The carpet of the suite squelches beneath your feet as you stand outside the door. The sound of running water is still coming from inside. Gingerly, you push the door open. The shower is running and there's nobody else in the en suite.

However, you spot something odd. A jerry can of gasoline is sitting on the floor by the toilet. A candle, burning quickly down to the wick, is wedged into the lid. You realise that the floor is covered in petrol and that the candle is about to drop its flame straight into the canister.

What next?

- You try to grab the candle before it reaches the gasoline

  (turn to page 29)

- You insist that the Royale Premiere is evacuated (turn to page 30)

- You tell the others and get out of the room as fast as you can

  (turn to page 31)

You leap forward to try and stop the open flame reaching the gasoline. You're not quick enough and it drops into the jerry can. The explosion rips through the whole hotel room, taking you, Walter and Carter with it.

You've taken a misstep, try a different decision by reassessing your actions with the candle on P28.

Pulling your authority as a police officer, you insist that Walter evacuates the hotel. He reluctantly agrees and you head downstairs to the main lobby.

An emergency is declared as the fire brigade appears to take care of the aftermath of the explosion. Guests, press, movie stars and staff all begin to file out into Sunset Boulevard outside and start to disperse. It only dawns on you now that the killer, if they were amongst them, now has a clear route of escape.

Before you can stop everyone and bring them back in, your superior arrives on the scene and questions what you've done. It's clear now that you're never going to catch the murderer or who was responsible for the explosion.

The case ends here for you. Evacuating the hotel was a mistake, try another decision that will keep the guests, stars and suspects all contained in the building on page 28.

'What?' Walter asks, his face slack.

You grab him by the arm and run for the door. Carter looks shocked as you both barrel towards him. Running as fast as you both can, you bundle into him and collapse out the door.

Behind you there's a brief flash and a bang as the candle finally burns down and connects with the gasoline. A gust of air washes over you, Walter and Carter. You catch your breath and pat yourself down, making sure you're still intact. The others are coughing and spluttering. Everyone is alive – it's a small miracle you managed to evade the explosion.

Your ears are ringing as you realise the explosion is over. Slowly, you stand back up and help the others to their feet.

'Oh, my god,' gasps Walter. 'What the hell was that?'

'I'm not an expert, but I think it was an explosion,' says Carter, covered in dust.

You all look back into von Hiltz's en suite. It's destroyed, the tattered shower curtain still aflame. There's broken glass all over the floor and the shattered toilet is spewing water across the tiles. The smell of gasoline is stronger than ever.

Staff and other guests appear along the corridor. Walter assures them that they are all okay. You suggest that the hotel is evacuated in case there are other booby traps set about the place.

'We can't do that!' Walter shouts. 'We're on the eve of the Golden Star Awards – it's the biggest night of the movie business. We can't evacuate people, we'll be ruined.'

You are still a little dazed and it takes you a moment to think. The other staff and some guests are all gawping at the huge hole in the side of the building left by the explosion.

'I think we should get ourselves checked out by the medics,' says Carter. 'I've got a terrible headache.'

~~~~~~~

You step into the charred remains of the room. The wind outside has picked up and is blowing in through the gaping hole, taking away some of the awful smell of petroleum with it. All the papers and clothes that were scattered about the room are now gone. The bathroom has been blown to pieces and there are little fires dotted about the place.

You manoeuvre yourself towards the en suite when something crunches under your foot. Looking down, you realise that you've stood on a picture frame, cracking the glass. You pick it up, you wipe away soot and dust from the surface. It reveals a signed picture of Blanche Aikerman, blowing a kiss towards the camera. Squinting, you try to decipher the message. It reads: '*To my darling Pete, thank you for everything, I'll never forget Cairo. Your love forever, Blanche x*'

Walter comes bumbling in behind you, coughing and gasping at the extent of the damage. He peers over your shoulder and you show him the picture.

'Ah yes, she really was a thing of beauty,' he says.

You ask if she was in a relationship with von Hiltz.

'Oh I couldn't possibly say.' He blushes, mopping his forehead with a handkerchief. 'You hear about these sorts of things in the gossip columns though, don't you?'

You remind him you're an officer of the law investigating a murder. And that you've both almost just been blown to smithereens.

'Herr von Hiltz and Ms Aikerman were … close, if I can be so bold,' says Walter. 'They aren't new guests to the Royale Premiere and we pride ourselves on keeping our mouths firmly shut about our guests. But I think they may have had a falling out over the last few days. Something seemed off about them. They ate at different times, in different parts of the hotel. It was as if they'd had some sort of lovers' tiff.'

You put the cracked picture down on the ground where you found it. Looking about the room, the place is a disaster. Knowing now that von Hiltz and Aikerman were possible lovers adds a new dimension to this investigation. Especially as the famed director has now disappeared and his room was rigged to blow. With two crime scenes in the hotel to handle, you have your work cut out for you.

Return to the scene of the crime or try to find out a bit more about von Hiltz. Where to next?

- You insist Walter takes you to the original crime scene

  (turn to page 47)
- You head down to the main lobby (turn to page 34)

It's only when you reach the main entrance of the Royale Premiere that you realise just how close you came to disaster in von Hiltz's room. One wrong step and you'd have gone up with the rest of the suite. Obliterated.

The fresh air outside the hotel is a welcome relief. The smell of the gasoline upstairs was giving you a headache. You need a moment to pull yourself together.

There's an electricity to the air throughout the hotel. People seem scared, frightened. But there's also a sense of dismissal, like explosions and near disasters happen all the time in this industry. You can't fathom showbusiness. This is your first foray into this world and it's already proven to be more odd, strange and downright bizarre than any other homicide you've ever worked.

Fire crews from the LAFD appear at the main entranceway. They hurry past you, shouldering their equipment. A clearing is made for them to go up and inspect the scene. You spot what looks like the chief of the operation and introduce yourself, flashing your badge. He rubs your cheek with his thumb and shows you the soot.

'Take it you were close to the action then, detective?' he asks with a smirk.

You tell him you were right in the middle of it all. And if you hadn't acted faster, they'd be sifting through your remains upstairs. He blows out his cheeks and whistles.

'Celebrities, huh?' he shrugs. 'Explosive lifestyles, quite literally. Let my boys take a look and make sure everything is secure. I take it you're not here for a social call or a cocktail with Blanche Aikerman.'

You remain tight-lipped and the chief takes the hint.

'I'll leave you to it, then,' he says, clapping you on the shoulder.

The chief heads into the hotel leaving you alone once more. Your thoughts turn to the explosion. There's no chance that whoever set that trap was targeting you – you've not been here long enough to warrant an enemy. The logical conclusion, then, is that Peter von Hiltz was the intended victim. Finding the elusive director becomes your top priority. You head back into the hotel and make a line for the front reception desk.

The whole area is chaos. Guests are clamouring for attention from the overworked staff. Everyone wants to know what's going on.

And the workers don't have a clue. You bypass the throng gathered around the long marble reception desk and snag a young man hurrying about like a headless chicken.

- You ask if von Hiltz has valet parked his car with the hotel staff

  (turn to page 36)

- You ask for a call to be made out for Peter von Hiltz over the

  public address system (turn to page 46)

'Eh, yes, he has,' says the young man. 'In fact, I think his car was just collected.'

You ask when.

'I think around the time of that loud bang from upstairs,' he says. 'Or, perhaps, before it. I'm not too sure. It's bedlam in here and I'm run off my feet.'

You ask where the valet parking garage is. The young man directs you through the back doors and into the bowels of the hotel. Hurrying as quickly as you can, you follow the signs that lead to the main garage of the Royale Premiere. Bursting through the doors, you find yourself on the main level of the car park.

Your sudden arrival startles a couple of the valet attendants. Grabbing a quick break, they stand up straight and ping away their cigarettes, dusting off their red velvet waistcoats. You grab the closest one, a young man with dark hair and bushy eyebrows. You ask him what's happened with von Hiltz's car.

'The director?' he asks. 'He was here just a couple of minutes ago. I think Joey went and fetched his car for him. He seemed in a rush, a bit short tempered. Or more so than usual. Why? What's up?'

You ask what he's driving.

'Ah, now that's the easy part,' says the attendant. 'Herr von Hiltz, he's one of our favourites, not because he's always in a bad mood but because of his ride. A superb, mint condition, just out of the wrapping Mercedes-Benz 190SL. Black, shining – convertible, of course – with a tan roof and interior. It's a thing of beauty, ain't it boys?'

He laughs as the others all flash you a thumbs-up.

'What I wouldn't give to have that car for a night,' says the attendant, his eyebrows arching. 'I was here when he arrived last night with Blanche Aikerman. I couldn't believe it when he pulled up and tossed me the keys. A beautiful car, a gorgeous dame, Man, some guys have all the luck, right? Meanwhile I'm stuck here with these greaseballs.'

A chorus of boos rains down on the attendant. He laughs and shrugs it off. A car pulls up in front of you. It's not a Mercedes, although it's still a rather handsome Buick. Another attendant climbs out, the keys spinning on his finger. With your car parked out front of the hotel, you need a set of wheels and fast. You snatch them from him and climb into the Buick.

'Hey!' he shouts. 'What's going on?'

You tell the valet parkers this is police business. You ask what direction von Hiltz headed in.

'South, I think,' says one of them. 'I reckon he was heading for the airport. He had luggage with him.'

That's enough for you to slam the door closed and stamp your foot on the gas pedal. You throw the Buick's big, heavy frame around the garage and out onto the main street outside. It handles like a boat as you weave it through the afternoon LA traffic, following signs for the airport. You keep your eyes peeled for the first sign of a Mercedes-Benz 190SL – racking your brain to try and remember what one of those looks like.

The sun is still high in the late afternoon sky. Everything feels scorched out here on the roads. The Royale Premiere is a relative dark hole compared to a Los Angeles day. You whizz through the traffic and find yourself on Sunset Boulevard. In the far distance you can see the Hollywood sign. It stands like a dishevelled, decrepit sentry, forever on guard over the city and Tinseltown. It's almost as if it knows what's happened to Blanche Aikerman and is looking to *you* to put things right.

You remember what the valet attendants said, that they thought von Hiltz would head south. Darting across traffic to the sound of honking horns, you get back on track. If von Hiltz *is* heading for the airport then you have to get there first. If he's able to make it on a plane, you'll never catch him.

You press down on the accelerator. Hard. The Buick's big, powerful engine responds, propelling you forward as you slice and dice between other motorists. There's no sign of the Mercedes or von Hiltz. You can't worry too long, you have to stay focused and reach LAX first.

The airport has been under renovation for the last few years. It's quickly becoming one of the most important and busiest transport hubs in all of the US. Needle in a haystack springs to mind. You follow the signs for the main terminal. As you round the corner, you spot something up ahead.

Von Hiltz's Mercedes stands out like a sore thumb among all the taxi cabs and civilian motors. It's sleek, dynamic, like a bullet on wheels. More importantly, you see the director himself climbing out, suitcase in hand.

You screech up the rampway and hurl the Buick into the drop-off zone. You're out the door and racing along the sidewalk before anyone can tell you off for abandoning the Buick at Arrivals. You burst through the doors of the LAX terminal and scan the place for von Hiltz. He's at the front of a queue, sunglasses still on, conversing with a Lufthansa clerk.

You shout his name. He snaps his head around, a sneer immediately creeping across his lips. He starts to run, pushing past other travellers and hurrying through the busy terminal. You give chase, drawing your pistol. You don't want to shoot him, you need answers. But you can't let him get away either. You shout for him to stop again but he ignores your request.

Some of the airport security have appeared. The commotion is enough to draw their attention. They spot you running with your gun and immediately draw their revolvers. They scream at you to stop and put down your weapon.

What do you do?

- You ignore them, pursuing von Hiltz (turn to page 39) ⬟
- You do as they say (turn to page 40) ⬟

You don't know where it comes from, but you hear the unmistakable crack of a gun going off. There are some screams and everyone in the terminal hits the floor. You keep running, until you feel your knees buckling underneath you.

Another crack, this time from ahead and you spill forward, your pistol spinning away across the well-polished floor. You try to get up but the feeling has gone from your legs. You roll over and find a large patch of blood forming in your chest. You've been shot, at least twice, once in the back, once in the front. Your breathing is growing erratic as you panic and your vital systems shut down. Hurried footsteps come thumping over to you. The faces of security staff from the airport fill your vision as you stare up at the ceiling.

Your eyelids are growing heavy and you can feel the cold, clammy touch of unconsciousness washing over you. As the world begins to turn dark, you hear one of the guards: 'Shit. We just killed a cop!'

You have been killed while pursuing a key witness in the case. Turn to page 38 when security demand you stop and rethink your next step.

You skid to a halt on the well-polished floor of the terminal building. The security personnel come running up to you. You angrily explain that you're a homicide detective and you show them your badge.

They immediately drop their guns. You tell them you're chasing a suspect and that they've got in your way. You point to von Hiltz who is almost at the other end of the terminal building. Everyone hurries after the director. He skips out of one of the doors at the end of the building that leads to the runways and hangars. You and the security staff do the same. As you adjust your eyes to the sunshine again, you see von Hiltz making good on his escape. You shout out his name.

It's enough to distract the director for a second. But the distraction proves fatal. He pauses, in the middle of a busy access road. A horn screams out from a baggage truck before it smashes into von Hiltz, sending him flying into the air. He crashes down hard a few feet away from the cart and rolls to a halt.

You race over to him. He's not moving. You roll him over so he's flat on his back. He's badly injured, leg sticking out at an unhealthy angle. Blood is running from his mouth. When he sees you, his eyes go wide. He grabs hold of your jacket lapels and pulls you in tight.

'Find who killed her,' he says, voice croaking, desperate. 'Find who killed my Blanche. Find them and kill them.'

His grip loosens. His eyes roll back in his head. He's gone, face contorted into a sad grimace.

'Damn,' says one of the airport security, the rest of the team catching up with you. 'He didn't see that damn truck coming. It just wiped him out.'

You close von Hiltz's eyes and stand up. You tell the security team they need to get an ambulance down here and your colleagues in the LAPD. This is now a crime scene.

'Hey, we can't close off the runway,' says one of them. 'We've got a busy airport to run.'

You keep your cool but firmly tell him that you're a homicide detective and this man was a suspect in a murder investigation. You're calling the shots.

'Hey, wait a minute,' says another guard. 'Isn't that Peter von Hiltz, the director?'

There's a hubbub as the group all huddle round to see von Hiltz's broken and twisted body. You bring them all back under control and remind them that they're professionals with a job to do. You don't want to have to haul them all down the station for interfering with an active investigation. That seems to do the trick and everyone snaps into action, stopping traffic and going to help the driver of the car that killed von Hiltz.

It's time to make a choice.

- You call Captain Barclay and explain what's happened at the

  airport (turn to page 42) ⭐

- You hail a cab, intending to head back to the Royale Premiere

  (to page 45) ⭐

'Von Hiltz!' your superior officer exclaims. 'The Kraut? He's dead? How the hell did that happen? And what are you doing at LAX? I thought you'd gone to the Royale Premiere!'

Keeping your voice low and making sure nobody can hear you, you quietly, efficiently and subtly tell Barclay what's happened, both here at the airport and to Blanche Aikerman. The line goes quiet. You're not sure if it's the phone or Barclay. Then your captain speaks up.

'Holy cow,' he says. 'This is *huge*!'

He makes some other customary curses and whistles, almost deafening you down the line. You suspected this would be the reaction when you eventually told Barclay what was going on. The man has a penchant for the dramatic. He was, as you understand it, a good cop in his day. But years as homicide captain, and with it all the glamour and profile that comes with working for the LAPD, have dulled his policework intuition. Barclay is a mercenary, a man on a mission to look after one thing and one thing only – himself.

When he's processed what's happened, his tone immediately changes.

'You did good, kid,' he says, clearing his throat. You think you can hear papers rustling in the background. 'You did real good.'

You say you're going to head back to the hotel.

'No, no, just stay where you are,' he says, hurriedly. 'Does anyone else in the department know about Blanche Aikerman?'

You confirm that it's only you and a handful of others at the hotel, her mother, the manager, that kind of thing.

'But no other cops?'

You confirm that's the case, wondering where this is going, a sinking feeling making your stomach churn.

'Okay, you did good, like I said. I'll take it from here.'

You protest, saying this is your case.

'And I'm taking over,' says Barclay. You can almost hear the dollar signs ringing in his eyes like a cash register. He's got the bug for fame and knows, immediately, what cracking a case of this magnitude could do for his reputation. If he catches the murderer in the process, that'll be an added bonus. Captain Barclay is in this for himself.

'You stay with the Kraut's body until the lab techs and photographer get there. This is huge, absolutely *huge*. Two of the biggest stars in Hollywood, dead, on my watch, on my turf. I'm going to be in every newspaper and magazine in the country tomorrow morning. Maybe even the world.'

You get the feeling Barclay is just talking to himself now. You make one last stab at protesting, saying that the case is yours, the call came through to *you* and you're the one who's been doing the legwork.

'Don't make this a disciplinary issue!' he screams down the phone. 'You do what *I* tell you. I'm your captain, after all, and the senior police officer. This is a serious, monumental case and the LAPD should put its best men on the job. Me. So you just sit there, keep your mouth shut, wait for the meat wagon to show up and get on with cleaning up the mess. I'm going to the Royale Premiere to straighten all this out. Got that?'

The phone goes dead. You're left there, listening to the dial tone. Slowly, you put the receiver back down and take a long, deep breath. Outside the doors of the terminal, you see that the ambulance has arrived for von Hiltz. There are other cops on the scene now too. You quickly realise then that this is where it all ends for you. You daren't go against Barclay's instructions, otherwise you'll be lucky to get a job as a crossing guard outside a school. The man has connections, serious connections to some of LA's less than savoury characters. And an ego to match that sense of invincibility that buckled cops tend to get when they can call in a favour from the gutter to City Hall and everywhere in between. His little black book has everyone's name in it, from the mayor to the lowliest of back-alley hoodlums and winos.

Thus ends your chance at catching Blanche Aikerman's killer. The case ends here for you. But you can always start again by turning to Chapter 1.

You're confident that the security team can hold the fort until some of your colleagues from the LAPD arrive. It's LA airport and it's the Goldies tomorrow night, so they'll hurry to get everything ironed out as more stars arrive. The cab driver takes you back to the hotel where things are starting to get busy. The afternoon sun has turned a rich orange and begun its descent towards the Pacific by the time you climb out of the cab and head into the main lobby.

Getting back to business, you feel that you need to speak with Mr Walter. He's the manager of the hotel and he has to be kept informed of everything that's going on. Von Hiltz's final words are still ringing in your head: 'find who killed my Blanche'. While you can't rule out that he is the murderer, the final words of a dying man, in your experience, aren't usually a lie. If von Hiltz did kill Blanche Aikerman, he's taken his reasons to his grave. You're not, however, convinced that's the case. And you need to speak with Walter the Royale Premiere manager.

Continue your line of inquiry on page 134.

The staff duly oblige. You stand and watch the chaos from a safe distance, waiting for von Hiltz to arrive. Five minutes pass. Then ten. Soon you've been waiting for half an hour. You ask the staff to put out another call. They do so and you wait another fifteen minutes. It's becoming apparent that this is a waste of time. Wherever von Hiltz is, he's not interested in answering.

Valuable time in the investigation has been wasted. You're about to do *something* when a member of the reception team flags you down. She holds up a phone.

'Detective, it's for you,' she says. 'It's your squad room, a Captain Barclay. He says it's urgent.'

That's all you need.

- You ignore the call (turn to page 179)

- You reluctantly take Captain Barclay's call (turn to page 70)

You tell Mr Walter that he is wasting time and that you have a crime scene to examine. He looks at Carter nervously and then concedes.

'Yes, of course, follow me please,' says Walter.

The hotel manager is nervous, sweat beading on his forehead. You sense there is a great unease about him that extends beyond the apparent murder of Blanche Aikerman.

'This is literally the *last* thing we needed,' he says. 'Today, of all days, just hours before the biggest night in Hollywood. I hope I can count on your candour and full confidentiality, officer. If something like this was to get out into the public, I think we might have a riot on our hands. You know how well thought of Blanche Aikerman was to the public, to the world even. To have lost her in this way, the night before her crowning glory, I'm not sure it would go down at all well.'

He stares off into the distance as you make your way up to the penthouse suite. As the elevator doors open, an older woman is slumped by the door, sobbing uncontrollably.

'Oh no,' says Walter, hurrying over to her side. 'Mrs Aikerman, I'm so, so sorry. Somebody should have been sent to fetch you.'

'My daughter! My beautiful daughter! She's been killed. She's been murdered by a monster. How can this have happened? Why?'

Walter tries to help Mrs Aikerman onto her feet but she's too weak. He snaps at Carter to help him and they lift her, taking her over to a small couch that's down the corridor a little away from the door of the penthouse suite.

What is your next move?

- You go to console a distraught Mrs Aikerman (turn to page 48)

- You immediately go to examine the crime scene (turn to page 50)

Mrs Aikerman is distraught. She blows her nose loudly into her handkerchief as she sits on the sofa, Mr Walter trying to comfort her. He sends Carter to fetch some brandy.

'My beautiful daughter, taken from us in the prime of her life,' says the old lady. 'She was an angel from heaven. The world will remember this day, I promise you. She was the most famous woman in the world and now she's gone. I'm all alone.'

'There, there, Mrs Aikerman, it's a shock to us all,' says Walter, holding her hand.

'I can't believe what's happened here. She was set to win big tomorrow night. She's always wanted one of those little gold statues. I remember she used to put on plays for us back at the farm in Iowa. We all couldn't believe how talented she was, even back then. Musicals, theatre, she was barely out of diapers. We all knew Blanche was going to be a star. And tomorrow night was going to be *her* night. Now look what's happened. She's dead, killed, murdered in cold blood right before her greatest moment. It's not fair, it's just not fair.'

She begins to sob uncontrollably again. Walter looks awkward as he tries, in vain, to comfort the grieving mother. Carter returns with a large goblet of brandy. He hands it to Mrs Aikerman who downs the drink with an expert swallow.

'I was just talking to her this morning,' she says. 'She was telling me about what dress she was wearing on the red carpet tomorrow night – something from Chanel. It had been sent all the way from Paris especially for the occasion. She wanted me to see her in it before the big night, to ask me what I thought, what adjustments it needed. I always helped her with that, she trusted me. My beautiful daughter, gone, gone!'

'There, there Mrs Aikerman,' says Walter.

'Perhaps she can wear it in her casket,' offers Carter.

Mrs Aikerman's mood changes in an instant. The devastated mother is now a snarling, furious monster, her eyes locked on the young waiter with icy rage.

'How dare you!' she screams. 'How dare you talk of my beautiful Blanche like that! Who do you think you are? You're a nobody, that's who, some street rat, trussed up in a waistcoat, that brings me drinks. Don't you know who I am? I'm the mother of the biggest movie star in the world! Get out of my sight!'

She hurls the empty glass at Carter with deceptive strength. He ducks and it smashes against the far wall.

'You heard the lady!' Walter shouts, too. 'Get out of here!'

Carter looks at you and shrugs.

'Guess I won't be getting a tip from any Aikerman today, huh?' he says and starts down the corridor.

Mrs Aikerman starts to cry again. Walter's face is bright red with rage as he tries to comfort her more.

Continue your hunt for the culprit on page 50.

You leave a grief-stricken Mrs Aikerman with Walter. The old lady is still sobbing as you ease your way in through the door of the penthouse apartment. A gentle breeze is wafting in through a set of double doors to your left. Peering over, you can see the outline of a bed. You head over to the bedroom and push the double doors open.

There, in front of you, is Blanche Aikerman. She's sprawled across the top of the bed, pale, lifeless. Her throat has been cut, neat and precise. As you round the bed, you take in as much as you can in these first few moments. Every murder investigation is a puzzle, an answer that's lying in front of you. A dead body can be the biggest clue you'll ever get when it comes to catching a killer. From the way the fatal blow has been inflicted to what the victim is wearing, these first impressions are *vital* to how you'll try and catch the killer.

Blanche Aikerman, even in death, is a beautiful woman. Everything about her seems otherworldly. She is, somehow, too attractive, too perfect to be from this planet. And for the first time you can see why the world's press, not to mention the cinema going public, see this actor. She is a star, born and bred.

Apart from the large gash across her throat, Blanche Aikerman remains the picture of Hollywood glitz and glamour. Her long evening gown is perfectly set across the top of the bed sheets. Her long, dark hair looks like it's just been styled, ready for the red carpet and her army of adoring fans. The pool of blood that's seeped from her throat has arched and absorbed into the bedlinen, almost like a halo. She is, quite frankly, the best-looking corpse you're ever likely to see.

And that's the problem. You've been to crime scenes before. Nothing has ever compared to this. From bums found in the back alleys of downtown LA to domestics in the slums, usually the stink of death is all around. Blanche Aikerman, however, has made something of a show of her own murder scene. That doesn't sit right with you. Whoever did this to her *knew* what they were doing. The chances of a fatal encounter, unplanned at that, can almost be completely ruled out.

You rub the back of your neck. The magnitude of what's happened is starting to sink in. The most famous woman in the world is lying dead in front of you. That's a problem. A *big* problem.

You take a deep breath. Looking about the bedroom, there's no obvious signs of a struggle. Everything in here is in its place, much like the rest of the suite. A tray of cold food is close by the bed, an open bottle of champagne sitting in an ice bucket. Then you realise something. The breeze, you can still feel it on the back of your neck. Despite the huge balcony doors being firmly closed.

Looking about, you try to find the source of the breeze. Then a knock at the bedroom doors distracts you.

'Good god,' says Mr Walter, turning pale as he spots Blanche Aikerman lying on the bed. 'That poor woman. Who could do such a thing?'

You throw him a stern look.

'Sorry, I just … I thought you should know that Mrs Aikerman has calmed down. I wondered if you wanted to have another word with her, perhaps give her an update on your investigation. She seems utterly distraught at what's happened to her daughter. We all are, of course.'

You need to make a decision here.

- You agree and go to speak with Mrs Aikerman (turn to page 54) 🔫

- You ignore Walter and carry on with examining Blanche Aikerman's bedroom and the source of the breeze

  (turn to page 52) 💋

'Yes, of course, I should leave you to it,' says Walter, backing out of the bedroom. He bows his head and closes the door.

You look around the place once more, trying to get a grasp as to what exactly has happened here. Blanche's body remains the centrepiece of the room. Inspecting her closely, you determine that this has all been done for show. The killer, whoever it may be, is meticulous, is capable of dressing and staging a scene. Ordinarily this would limit the amount of suspects there could be. But with a hotel full of industry types, there's no shortage of flair for the dramatic.

There's only so much you can tell at this stage. Forensics will have to determine the true cause of death. But the blood seeping from the wound in Blanche's throat appears fresh, bright red, glistening in the fading sunlight seeping in through the balcony doors. There's a serenity to her face, almost a smile there too. No signs of struggle, her fingernails are intact. That means there's a very good chance she knew who her murderer was.

You're sweating. The pressure is mounting. Oh, to be a cop.

Then you feel the breeze on the back of your neck. It makes the sweat cold and you remember what you noticed from before. There's air coming from somewhere, somewhere you can't place. It seems like a little thing. But if experience has taught you anything, the little things in murder investigations can lead to big things.

You look about the bedroom. No windows are open, the balcony doors are firmly shut. The en suite has no window and the door has been closed by Mr Walter. That leaves only one place. A small grille in the wall high above Blanche Aikerman's bed – the hotel air-conditioning duct. You're no expert in these systems, but you're certain that it's not supposed to be so cold, or so powerful. There's something not right.

Climbing up on the bedside table, it's tall enough to help you reach the vent. You manoeuvre yourself carefully so as not to disturb Blanche's body or the rest of the crime scene. Then you notice that the grille has been dislodged. It's not sitting flush with the wall, as it should be. Cool air is seeping out through the gap. You jiggle the grille free and peer inside the vent. There, staring back at you, is something you were *not* expecting – a bloody knife.

You reach in and carefully free the blade from the vent, making sure you don't get your fingerprints on the handle. The blood on the knife is still fresh. You're not a scientist and you can't assume that this is the murder weapon. The lab will be able to confirm everything. However, you'll never look a gift horse in the mouth. And it's not a stretch of the imagination to think that this knife in your hand is what caused Blanche Aikerman's demise.

Carefully stepping down from the bed, you make your way out of the bedroom and towards the front door of the suite. Walter is waiting on the other side, nervously fiddling with the cuffs of his blazer, a little moustache above his top lip twitches. Before he can react, there's a scream from Mrs Aikerman, still sitting on a sofa a little further down the hallway.

'Oh, my god!' she yells.

Only then do you realise that you're holding the bloody knife in plain view of everyone. Perhaps this wasn't your best idea, and you try to cover it up as best you can.

Proceed with your investigation on page 54.

'Is that … is that what I think it is?' she gasps.

You quickly hide the blade in the pocket of your trench coat. She holds a handkerchief to her mouth, shocked. You apologise for the shock and state that you have no evidence that this is the murder weapon involved in her daughter's killing. But you'll have to call in your lab techs to run analysis over it and the crime scene.

Mrs Aikerman seems to be a little placated. Mr Walter tuts loudly, disapproving of your lack of subtlety. You can hardly blame him, this was something of a mistake. You should have anticipated that Mrs Aikerman was still close by. Slowly, Mrs Aikerman, a short woman with a neat frame and sharp eyes, calms down. She stares blankly ahead of her, lost in thought. Her hands are trembling, the veins a pale blue against her ashen white, thin skin. When she sees you approach, she tries to sit up properly, pushing a loose strand of her heavily dyed hair away from her face.

'I'm sorry about earlier,' she says. 'As you can imagine, this has been a terrible shock. Blanche was my world, she was everything. She looked after me, never left me aside, even as she became more and more famous. She still had time for her old mom. And I *am* old, officer, look at me. Look at my hands!'

She holds her hands out in front of her for you to look at. They're still trembling. Expensive rings adorn every finger. A diamond the size of a large pebble particularly catches your eye. It's worth more than a decade's worth of your salary.

'I'm weak and frail now and I used to be so strong,' says Mrs Aikerman. 'Hank, Blanche's dad, was never around when she was growing up. He liked his friends too much to ever play the father role. The lazy son of a bitch was never in work either, it was left up to me to keep a roof over our heads. We came from nothing, officer, absolutely nothing. Some backwater town in Milwaukee. Then he gets up one morning and says he's going over to fight the Nazis, says he's had enough of what's been going on over there and that it's "time to do his duty". You'd think he was Uncle Sam himself the way he was talking. I didn't believe it of course. No doubt he owed somebody money and wanted to skip town for a couple of weeks or months and leave me to deal with his mess. That's the last either of us ever heard of him. I doubt he even made it to the recruitment station. He was dumb as a lame mule, even on a good day. And that was us, just the two of us, Blanche and me against the world.'

She sniffs. Then something changes in her. It's just a flash, a second, but you pick up on an anger there, lurking behind her watery eyes. It could be bitterness or it could be shock. But it's something. You offer her your handkerchief and she gladly takes it. Opening her handbag, she pulls out a purse. Inside is a tattered, tired old photograph of a young woman and a little girl.

'This is us on her eighth birthday,' says Mrs Aikerman. 'I can't remember who took that picture, it certainly wasn't Hank, I can tell you that much. He wouldn't have known Blanche's birthday if it came up and slapped him across the face. We had such a wonderful time that day. She put on a show for the rest of the family and her friends. She was always doing that, singing, dancing, putting on plays, you name it. She was born to be a star, born to be in showbusiness. And what a star she became. We showed them, officer, we showed *everyone* who ever doubted us. Blanche lit up the screen and the stage every time she appeared on it. People couldn't take their eyes off her, even if they wanted to. This was supposed to be her big moment Now look what's happened.'

Mrs Aikerman begins to cry again. You try to console her but she waves you away.

'I'm sorry, it's just … it feels like such a terrible loss, not just to me, but to the whole world,' she says. 'Can you imagine that? One person being snatched away and all the people on the planet feeling the loss. That's what this will be, I assure you, mark my words. I want you to find whoever did this and I want you to kill *them*.'

A madness falls over the elderly woman. She grabs your lapels and pulls you in close.

'Find them,' she rasps at you. 'Find them and you kill them, you can do that, you're a cop. You can kill them and nobody will know the difference. The world will thank you for it, officer, believe me. You'll be a hero, a celebrity in your own right, an overnight hit, like our Blanche. It's what we all want, it's *justice*.'

Her grip on the lapels of your raincoat is iron-like. She's staring at you, eyes wide. Before you can try and free yourself, somebody clears their throat a little further up the corridor.

'Excuse me, Mrs Aikerman,' says Carter. 'I've got that other brandy for you.'

The appearance of the young waiter is enough to distract the old woman and she lets go of you. She composes herself and snaps her fingers, reaching out for the glass from Carter. He gives you a sly look as he retreats back down the hallway, leaving Mrs Aikerman with her drink.

'I'm sorry, officer,' she says to you. 'I don't know what's come over me these past few hours. I feel like the world is on fire and I can't do anything about it. I used to have so many ideas, be in charge. I looked after Blanche's affairs for her, was her manager, her representative. But recently, my mind isn't what it used to be. And that snake von Hiltz has been ambling to push me out of the picture more and more. But Blanche always looked after me, the way I looked after her when her father left. What am I going to do now that she's gone, huh? What am I going to do now?'

The mention of the elusive director reminds you that you should speak with others close to Blanche Aikerman before the news of her death gets out. You reassure Mrs Aikerman that you're doing your best and that the murderer will face the full extent of the law as and when they are caught.

'I've heard it all before, officer,' she says sadly to you. 'When you get to my age, you lose faith in the authorities. Justice is for the rich and powerful. And while my daughter was wealthy, she was still nothing in this industry. A body, a look, a piece of meat. Victor Ramsay at Thundersaga Pictures, he knows all about that. You speak to him, officer, and you'll find your killer. Believe me.'

You thank Mrs Aikerman again for her time, Walter the hotel manager steps out of the penthouse suite and locks the door behind him. You head for the elevators.

- Continue your investigation at the Royal Premiere Hotel by turning to page 62 turning to page 62

- Carry on digging into von Hiltz and his past on page 27 on page 27

You hurry past Mrs Aikerman, trying your best to hide the knife. It's caused enough consternation for you and the old lady. You reach the elevators and press the button to take you straight down to the lobby.

The blade feels heavy in your pocket. Unnaturally heavy. You know it's just your imagination playing tricks on you. But you can't help but feel like you're in the *Tell Tale Heart* by Edgar Allan Poe. The knife, the murder weapon – or possible murder weapon – is almost calling out to you from inside your jacket. This isn't your first murder scene. And it's not your first murder weapon. It is, however, your first celebrity murder victim. The idea that this is the knife that killed the most famous woman in the world is strangely overpowering. A piece of history, not just Hollywood history, but *real* history is right there, tucked away in your coat pocket, just out of sight. Never out of mind though.

The elevator doors open. The busy lobby of the Royale Premiere is staring back at you. The noise, the people, it's a welcome distraction. Being left alone with your thoughts and the knife in your pocket was quite overwhelming. The hubbub of the busy hotel is enough to set you thinking straight.

Now that there's a murder weapon, you feel that it's the right time to call in the forensics technicians. You've examined the crime scene, made sure it's secure, now you can get the rest of the team in here. Again, you'll be a little relieved. While you've only been here a short while, the pressure of the case has been immense. Greater than anything else you've ever faced before. Blanche Aikerman wasn't just another body in an alleyway, in the wrong place at the wrong time, the victim of a domestic situation gone wrong. She was a star, a famous celebrity, a woman with the world at her feet. Knowing that you've been out here, operating on your own like some Wild West marshal, it's taken its toll. You don't think anyone else would feel any different.

You take a deep breath and head over to the main reception desk. The staff are busy, processing a long queue of impending guests and other dignitaries. Everything is expensive and valuable looking, from the six-inch heels to the flowers in wide-brimmed hats.

You flag down one of the reception team. Flashing your badge, you ask if there's a staff safe. The young man nods. You walk around the reception desk and into a small office directly behind the busy front area. He shows you the safe and opens it with the code. You kneel down and, making sure the knife is still wrapped in your handkerchief, you place it in the safe. You thank the staff member and he locks it away.

Heading back out into the main reception area, you start to think about your next move. That's when you spot him. Victor Ramsay – studio executive at Thundersaga Pictures, where Blanche Aikerman was a star.

He's not somebody you know directly. But he's almost as famous as the actors, producers and directors he employs. The pictures in the newspapers and film reels don't do the mogul justice. He is, in real life, much larger than anything you could have imagined.

Well over six feet tall and almost the same in width, he walks with a commanding confidence, every step shudders the ground. His suit is huge, acres of fabric cut, sliced and stitched together in the latest fashion. It's the only part of him that appears human, everything else is enlarged and, strangely, grotesque. From his bulging eyes and the slab of meat for a head to his pursed lips, slightly blue, and comically small ears, Victor Ramsay barrels across the lobby of the Royale Premiere like the *Titanic* on its maiden voyage.

You think of Blanche, not as the global superstar she has become, but as a young woman trying to make it in an industry dominated by men like Ramsay. You try to imagine what challenges she faced, that sheer intimidation factor these executives must hold over young and aspiring actors. You're a cop, in L.A., and you find him daunting. What must others be like in his presence? You wonder how much Ramsay knows.

You have two choices here, you hurry to catch up with Ramsay (turn to the next page) or you can catch up with the forensics team before you head down to the lobby to hunt out Victor Ramsay of Thundersaga Pictures on page 62.

'Can I help you?' he asks.

Ramsay is even larger when you get up close to him. It feels like you're staring up at a mountain. You flash your badge. His tone doesn't change. There's an intimidation about him but it's only from his sheer size. His voice is controlled, his manner polite.

'Is something wrong, officer?' he asks.

You decide that this is far too public a place to be conducting this kind of conversation. Although the Moon would still be too small a space to speak with someone like Victor Ramsay. You politely usher him away from the peering queue at reception to a quieter alcove further in the lobby.

Turn to page 64 to see how your conversation goes.

The lobby of the Royale Premiere hotel is awash with people. There's a buzz to the air, an excitement as everyone seems to be in a mad rush getting from one side of the building to the other. Outside the main doors, lavish cars and limousines are lining up as more and more exclusive guests and Hollywood's leading players arrive for the awards tomorrow night.

In all the hurly burly, it's hard to distinguish one face from the other. You recognise some people straight away. There's Dirk McMichaels, leading man and star of countless westerns. Meanwhile Clive Brookfield, fresh off his successful turn as a Chicago gangster in a prohibition movie, is smoking a Cuban cigar at the entrance of the hotel bar. Not far from him is Mary Moore, a femme fatale famous for her bedroom eyes and long mane of black hair, dark as an LA midnight. If you remember rightly, she's about to play Joan of Arc in an upcoming biopic.

Everyone, it seems, is here except for the man you're looking for. You don't know a lot about him, only that he's one of Hollywood's most influential studio executives. His name is often featured in newspapers and trade magazines, pictured beside big actors as they sign huge deals for millions of dollars. He's a hit maker but reclusive. Finding him here in the Royale Premiere is like a needle in a haystack.

You decide to use all the privileges that come along with being a member of the LAPD and head for the main reception desk. Long queues are snaking out from the well-polished marble, the staff hurriedly trying to keep tempers from fraying. There are a few red faces and steely looks as you head straight to the top of the line, badge in hand.

A young woman, flushed but still smiling, greets you. You introduce yourself and ask if an announcement can be put out through the public address system for Victor Ramsay. She duly obliges.

'Mr Ramsay ... Mr Victor Ramsay. Could you please report to the main reception desk. There is an urgent message for you.'

You thank the staff member and take a step to one side. The announcement seems to have set tongues wagging up and down the long lines of waiting guests and patrons. You watch them all very carefully, looking for any reactions. There's nothing out of the ordinary, from what you can tell. Hotel announcements and a big Hollywood player are commonplace in this town.

Then you spot him. He's hard to miss. The pictures in the newspapers and film reels don't do the mogul justice. He is, in real life, much larger than anything you could have imagined.

Well over six feet tall and almost the same in width, he walks with a commanding confidence, every step feeling like it shudders the ground. His suit is huge, acres of fabric cut, sliced and stitched together in the latest fashion. It's the only part of him that appears human, everything else is enlarged and, strangely, grotesque. From his bulging eyes and slab of meat for a head to his pursed lips, slightly blue, and comically small ears, Victor Ramsay barrels across the lobby of the Royale Premiere like the *Titanic* on its maiden voyage.

'There's a message for me,' he says, voice unnaturally loud.

The young woman who helped you, tiny in his shadow, points over at you. Ramsay cocks an eyebrow and shuffles to the edge of the reception area.

'Can I help you?' he asks.

You flash your badge. His tone doesn't change. There's an intimidation about him but it's only from his sheer size. His voice is controlled, his manner polite.

'Is something wrong, officer?' he asks.

You decide that this is far too public a place to be conducting this kind of conversation. Although the Moon would still be too small a space to speak with someone like Victor Ramsay. You politely usher him away from the peering queue at reception to a quieter alcove further in the lobby.

Turn the next page to see what Ramsay has to say ...

'What can I help you with, officer?' Ramsay asks you.

He seems calm, relaxed, not at all phased by the prospect of speaking with the police. Even as the whole hotel whispers and gossips around you both, the movie mogul is unshaken. You sense that he is a man who is used to getting his own way. Apart from his physical prowess, he has a demeanour about him, an unflappable confidence that can only exist when he's used to winning. Talking with a detective in a busy hotel lobby is childsplay to him.

That's why you have to be clever. You don't want to give away too much. It would be valuable to work out what *he* knows first. You are polite and mention that you're conducting routine enquiries about a complaint.

'And what, exactly, does that have to do with me?' he asks with a casual smile. 'In case you haven't noticed, officer, we're getting ready for the Golden Star Awards here. I've got actors and staff flying in from the four corners of the planet to be here and they all want to speak with me about something or other. You made a request of me, now you tell me it's for something "routine", really? I don't have the time, I'm afraid.'

The savvy confidence that's made Ramsay one of Hollywood's leading executives is on full display here. He's keeping his cards close to his chest, offering nothing that might indicate he knows what's happened to Blanche. You decide to press him a little further and ask about his leading lady.

'Oh yes, she's a wonderful talent, but then again, so are *all* of the actors who work for me, officer,' he says, raising an eyebrow. 'You see, Thundersaga Pictures has a reputation in this town, and beyond, for that matter. We make quality movies that the public loves. Two very high accolades, I'm sure you'll agree. And it's up to me, as chief executive, to make sure that those accolades keep coming. You see, I'm something of a stickler for how my actors and my staff conduct themselves. They represent the company, with what they say and what they do. That's from your top-billed stars like Blanche Aikerman to the boy who fetches my newspapers in the morning. I expect them *all* to buy in to the Thundersaga mantra – top quality, all of the time.'

You ask if he holds *himself* to that same standard.

'Of course I do,' he says, his face flushing a little. 'I'm the captain of the ship, officer. I can't expect the rest of the company to adhere to standards I won't stick to myself. I learned that in the army.'

You probe a little further into his military background. Ramsay looks around a little, it's the first time he's seemed phased. He places a hefty paw on your shoulder.

'Really, officer, it was a long time ago now,' he says, much quieter than before.

You insist, reminding the mogul that you're a LAPD detective, carefully omitting that you're from the homicide department. Ramsay falters for a moment, then a big smile returns to his huge face, as if he's remembered his script.

'I was at Omaha Beach, that's in France,' he says, casually, still smiling. 'I was with the Sixteenth Infantry Regiment, we stormed the beach and knocked the Nazis for six. Four of the worst years of my life. You don't get an easy time of it when you're a man of my stature. Everybody thinks you're a tough guy. And that's just your own comrades. What the Germans tried to do to me is even worse. But I'm a man of means and the things I learned in the army have stuck with me throughout my life. And when I came home, I headed out west and here I am now. Not too bad for a country boy from Iowa, eh, officer?'

You agree with him. Ramsay straightens his tie. He looks around the lobby of the hotel. There are still prying eyes, everyone wondering what the great Victor Ramsay is talking about to a police officer. He clears his throat.

'Is there anything else, officer?' he asks.

He's not going to offer up anything else on his own.

You can either reveal more to Ramsay or pursue another line of enquiry. What's your next step, detective?

- You tell Ramsay about Blanche Aikerman's murder (turn to the next page)

- You wonder what's happened to Peter von Hiltz (turn to page 73)

'Good god,' says Ramsay.

The movie mogul's face goes slack. He appears to be a little unsteady on his feet. You reach out to try and steady him but you realise there's nothing you can do. If this giant of a man wants to fall, he's going to do it. And probably squash you underneath him.

'I'm fine,' he says, leaning against the wall and catching his breath. 'It's just … that's ghastly news. I can't believe it. Are you sure she's dead?'

You confirm that Blanche Aikerman is dead. Murdered, even.

'Murdered? You can't be serious? Blanche Aikerman. *The* Blanche Aikerman?'

This is becoming a running trend when you break the news of her death. You reassure Victor Ramsay that your information is accurate and that you're conducting a murder investigation.

'What terrible news.'

He seems to fall into deep thought for a moment. His balance returns and he focuses on you, staring down from his enormous height.

'Do you have any suspects?' he asks.

You tell him that you're in the process of conducting your enquiries.

'Good. I have some very dear friends in the Los Angeles Police Department. You all do sterling work and I'm certain you'll catch whoever did this to dear Blanche. Tell me something, officer, was she murdered recently?'

You tell Ramsay that the pathology team hasn't had a chance to examine the crime scene yet. But they will. Once that happens, they can determine a time of death or close to it. You ask him why he's curious.

'Just shock, I suppose. I spoke with her only yesterday,' he says. 'She's been a great champion of my studio, Thundersaga Pictures. In fact, our last five years have only been successful *because* of Blanche Aikerman and her work with Peter von Hiltz.'

You ask if Ramsay has seen the director.

'No, can't say I have,' he says. 'Which is odd given the contract I've just offered the pair of them. A golden handcuffs deal, strictly confidential, of course. Although if I can't trust a police officer then who can I trust, eh?'

He laughs, the fat beneath his chin wobbling like a walrus.

'I shouldn't laugh,' he says, correcting himself. 'This is a sad time. A sad time indeed. Not just for the studio but for the whole of Hollywood, the world in fact. It couldn't have come at a worse time for both of them.'

You ask why Blanche's death would affect von Hiltz.

'It was a two-for-one offer, in a manner of speaking,' says Ramsay. 'I offered them more money than they could count, locking them into working solely for me at Thundersaga for the next decade. They would have had complete creative control to make whatever pictures they wanted. But the deal was for *both* of them. If von Hiltz said no and Blanche agreed then the deal was off. I wasn't about to break up one of the most lucrative and successful partnerships in showbusiness. It was all or nothing, it said so in black and white in the contract I gave him to deliver to her.'

You're starting to see that there has been more to von Hiltz's involvement with Blanche's affairs than first appeared. You ask if they were romantically involved.

'I couldn't tell you,' he says. 'I had a strictly business-only relationship with both of them. I like to keep a distance, officer, make sure I can't ever be compromised on feeling or emotion with the people I work with and have work for me. It's better that way, I find. Thundersaga movies have topped the charts with critics and the public for almost two decades running. You don't get on in this biz by knowing the ins and outs of everyone's personal lives, let me tell you that much.'

Ramsay checks his watch. It's clear that he's offered up all that he wants to. You thank him for his time, remembering what Mrs Aikerman said to you. As he's about to leave, you ask him his thoughts on what she said.

'Petra Aikerman is an old woman,' he says, smiling. 'As I've told you before, I don't dirty my hands or sully my reputation with the personal lives of actors or their mothers, officer. Mrs Aikerman is entitled to think what she wants, this is a free country, last I checked. And if she has a problem with me then she knows where to find me – Burbank, my office is above the soundstage that bears my name. You can't miss it. She knows where it is, she was in there often enough picking up cheques for her daughter. I'll be waiting.'

Victor Ramsay sets off again across the lobby of the hotel. The crowd moves out of his way as he goes, cruising like a liner from New York on its way to England. Before you can digest everything that he's just said, the young woman at reception calls over to you.

'Officer, it's your squad room, an urgent call,' she says.

- You ignore the call and follow your line of inquiry with

  Ramsay on page 181
- You take the call (turn to the next page)

'What the hell is going on down there?'

It's Captain Barclay, your superior officer back at the squad room. He must have returned to the station house sometime after you left. Clearly, he lost his round of golf with the mayor or the chief. He sounds angry, although he *always* sounds angry. Being a homicide captain in a town like Los Angeles isn't an easy gig. Far from it. This time, though, he seems particularly irked with you.

'Where the hell have you been all afternoon? Don't you realise how busy the city is this weekend? I need every pair of hands I can, here, in the station.'

You look about the reception area. It's still incredibly busy. You don't want to speak too loudly. If you do, the wrong set of ears might eavesdrop some vital information, namely the untimely demise of Blanche Aikerman.

You try to skirt around the subject. Reminding Captain Barclay that you got a call from the hotel that abruptly hung up, you say you're chasing some leads.

'Wait a minute,' he says.

There's a flutter of papers in the background. You wait while the captain gets his thoughts together.

'Did you say the Royale Premiere?' he asks. 'That's where the Golden Star Awards are taking place aren't they?'

You confirm that is the case.

'We've been getting a couple of calls from some of the hacks around there,' he says. 'In fact, the switchboard says it's like the Fourth of July down there. That there has been a flurry of phone calls from reporters asking if something is going on in the hotel. You wouldn't know anything about that, would you?'

Your heartbeat is racing. The pressure was already great when you realised that Blanche Aikerman had been killed. Now you have the captain breathing down your neck. The last thing anyone needs is a panic. And as soon as the news gets out that the world's most famous actress has been murdered, all hell will break loose. Any chance of catching the killer, if they're still here, will be gone.

Then something pops into your head. It's a long-lost memory, one of those little tidbits of information from your days at the police academy. Something so innocent but useful that it's just been waiting to be used for a long, long time. You whisper into the phone and hope that Captain Barclay remembers it, too.

'Zotzed?' he replies.

You panic, thinking that you've remembered your code words and slang all wrong. Then Captain Barclay catches up.

'Are you dealing with a murder, officer?'

You confirm it's the case. You can almost hear the cogs turning in the captain's head from across the city.

'And the victim, are they … famous?' he asks.

You confirm again. Barclay whistles down the phone, almost deafening you.

'How important are we talking about here?'

You try to keep your voice as low as possible. There's no way you can mention Blanche Aikerman's name, you don't know who is listening. Even the line might be tapped by some nosy housekeeper. You try your best to paint as loose a picture as possible while keeping everything vague and non-descript.

'Do you want the forensics team to come take a look?' asks Barclay.

You say yes. And that it might be prudent if he joins them. This is going to be big, much bigger than anything you've handled recently. Or ever, for that matter.

'All right,' says the captain, 'I'll be there as quick as I can.'

Before he goes, however, you stress the art of subtlety. Captain Barclay was a good cop, or so you've been led to believe. But since he rose through the ranks of the LAPD and landed the cushty number of homicide captain, he's taken to something of the dramatic entrance. He only takes cases he knows will get his name in the headlines. And if he knew the enormity of this one, he'd be frothing at the mouth already – swooping in on a helicopter and making sure the cameras were all turned on him.

You ask him and the lab technicians to meet you at the service entrance around the back of the hotel. You'll be able to take them to the crime scene from there without too much fuss.

'Give us thirty minutes,' he says. 'And don't touch anything until we arrive. This sounds like it's important.'

He hangs up before you can say goodbye. You replace the receiver and turn back to face the busy lobby of the hotel. With

Captain Barclay's warning not to touch anything at the crime scene still ringing in your ears, you face a direct choice.

What will it be?

- You wonder what's happened to Peter von Hiltz

(turn to the next page)

- You make your way to the back entrance of the hotel and wait for Captain

Barclay and the forensics team (turn to page 74)

You ask the friendly reception staff if they've seen the elusive director. They all look at each other. There's a hesitation there. When you ask what's the matter, the woman who handed you the phone blushes a little.

'Herr von Hiltz is … not the easiest guest we've ever had to serve here at the hotel, detective,' she says. 'If any of us had seen him, we'd remember exactly where and when.'

'And we'd know how to get out of his way,' says a young bellhop, his face covered in acne. 'You don't want to be the one who gets on his wrong side, especially when he's angry.'

'Which is all the time,' she adds.

'And his tips are lousy,' he says.

There are a few disapproving tuts.

'What?' the young bellhop shrugs. 'It's true.'

A picture of von Hiltz is forming in your head. You decide you should check out his suite and ask the staff where he is staying. They give you the room number and you head for the elevators through the busy crowd.

When you reach the floor, to your surprise, you find Mr Walter and Carter from earlier lingering around a door. Even before you count down the numbers, you realise they are outside von Hiltz's suite.

Continue your investigation into von Hiltz on page 27.

You weave your way through the throng of people within the main building of the hotel. More famous faces are appearing every minute as everyone gears up for the big awards. The staff are starting to look more frantic and there's an excitement in the air, tinged only with the faintest scent of apprehension.

The implications of Blanche Aikerman's death start to weigh heavy on your mind. You begin to wonder what this place will be like when the news breaks. And it *will* break. There's no doubt about that. You've done well to keep a lid on the murder up until now. But with every passing moment, the chances of it leaking, of the press finding out, or somebody in the business, become more realistic.

The worry drives you on. You make your way through the hotel towards the back corridors and the side of the Royale Premiere that the general public never gets to see. You push through a door marked 'staff only' and into the dingy corridors and hallways of the underbelly of the hotel. Making your way through the maze, you spot directions to the back loading bay. Following the corridor, you reach a door at the end. As you go to push the handle, the door flies open and whacks you in the face.

Stunned, you stumble back. The biting pain spreads across your face as you realise your nose is probably broken. Coughing and spluttering, you try to compose yourself. Your eyes are watering, but you can just about make out a figure standing by the door. As you pull yourself together, you wipe your eyes and find the elusive director Peter von Hiltz is staring at you.

Before you can react, before you can even catch your breath, von Hiltz takes off. He shoves past you and bolts back down the corridor. There's no time to waste. You give chase.

The director is fast, much faster than his appearance would dictate. He has a good headstart but you're on him, keeping him in sight. Von Hiltz shoulders a door open and slams it closed behind him, hoping to slow you down. You barge your way through, not missing a step.

The director hurries around a corner and begins climbing a set of stairs. You cry out to him, demanding he stops but he ignores you. Bounding up the stairs two at a time, you cut the distance between you down. Sensing you close behind him, von Hiltz makes a quick turn and shoves his way through another door. You follow him, close behind now. He's flagging, the speed evaporating from his legs. He throws worried looks over his shoulder as he hurries down a hallway, this one much more lavish and decorated than the others hidden behind the scenes.

You cry out to him again, insisting he has nowhere to go. Clutching his side, von Hiltz is almost finished. His feet begin to drag on the carpet and he's almost at a standstill. You're about to reach out for him when he does something unexpected.

Reaching into the inside of his jacket, he pulls out a pistol. You have split seconds to think.

- You stop and hold up your hands, hoping to reason with the

  director (turn to the next page)

- You dive forward and tackle von Hiltz before he can pull the

  trigger (turn to page 77)

Von Hiltz looks at you, his face flushed, hair matted against his sweaty forehead. You hold up your hands, trying to show you don't mean him any harm. He's panting for breath, the pistol trained at your head, your chest, the barrel shaking in his hands.

'I didn't kill her,' he says to you in his thick, German accent. 'I didn't have anything to do with her death. It wasn't me, you have to understand that.'

You remain silent. A million questions are running through your mind as you stare down the barrel of von Hiltz's pistol. Slowly, you try to move forward, hoping to catch him off-guard and maybe wrestle the gun from him. He spots you moving and locks his eyes on yours.

'I'm sorry it had to be this way,' he says.

He pulls the trigger. Two loud booms feel like they've made the whole world shake. He turns and slowly runs away down the corridor. You try to pursue him, but you can't. Every morsel of your body is frozen, feeling like a dead weight. You can't move.

You look down at your chest. Two large patches of blood are expanding across your shirt. You realise then that his aim was perfect. It's too late to do anything about it now.

You fall to your knees and keel over onto your side. The last thing you see before the world turns dark, is Peter von Hiltz running away down the corridor. His words echo in your mind. *'I'm so sorry it had to be this way.'*

The case ends for you here, after misjudging von Hiltz. Remember your police training and perhaps rethink your approach to a suspect pointing a gun at you on the previous page.

The director isn't fast enough for you. He's too tired, too exhausted from the chase. You smash your shoulder into his jaw and you both go tumbling down onto the floor. He lets out a wail of pain and your limbs are entangled. The pistol has bounced away somewhere out of reach. That suits you as you fancy your chances in a fistfight with von Hiltz.

Using the chaos and confusion, you aim a well-practised punch into the director's gut. He wheezes and rolls over as you get to your feet. Pulling your own gun from inside your trench coat, you aim it at the director. As he hears the safety click, he realises the game is up.

'All right, all right, don't shoot me,' he says, doubled over on the floor and clutching his belly. 'I give up.'

You help him to his feet and push him against the wall. Frisking him for other weapons, he's clean. Turning him around, he stares at you, face flushed red, hair matted with sweat and stuck to his forehead. You ask him why he ran.

'Because you're the law,' he says bitterly. 'If there's one thing I've found living here in America, it's that a man with a German accent is automatically found guilty of even the most petty crime. Even someone as powerful as me has to deal with wretched prejudice. I'd ask you if you know what it's like to live that kind of way, but I know you don't. Nobody does. Nobody asks what I did in the war because people have made up their minds already. They want me hung, drawn and quartered before I even open my mouth.'

You tell him you're not interested in executing him, unless he's done something wrong. And that by pulling a gun on a LAPD officer and avoiding questioning, it makes him look guilty as hell. Even if he *hasn't* opened his mouth.

'You're right, I shouldn't have done that,' he says. 'It's just … since Blanche was murdered, I feel like every pair of eyes is on me, like everyone is out to get me. And for nothing. I had nothing to do with what happened to her. You have to believe me.'

As far as you know, nobody other than yourself, Mr Walter, the waiter and Mrs Aikerman know that Blanche has been killed. You put this to Peter von Hiltz.

The director bows his head. He begins to cry, his shoulders bobbing up and down.

'I saw her,' he said. 'I saw her, lying in that state, her throat cut, blood everywhere. I saw her. She was just lying there, a corpse, a beautiful corpse, reduced to nothing. The most famous woman in the world and now she is nothing.'

You tighten your grip on von Hiltz and press him. He clears his throat, wiping the tears from his cheeks.

'Before the waiter found her, I saw her, just lying there,' he says. 'Ramsay, at Thundersaga, he offered us both a new contract. A golden-handcuffs deal that would tie me and Blanche to the studio for the future. It was more money than we could count, truckloads of dollars, to stay exclusively with him and keep making the hits we've become known for. And I wanted the deal, I wanted it badly. My imagination, it's nothing like anyone else on this planet, believe me. The things I can see when I close my eyes, the epics, the masterpieces, they make my *Boudica*, my *Tragedy of the Titanic* look like film-student projects for class. This was my chance, my shot at becoming Hollywood's greatest ever director. But Ramsay wanted us both, me and Blanche or no deal. One wasn't enough, he had to have us both. So, I took the deal to her, the contract, and she laughed in my face. She knew she had me where she wanted me, that she was finally calling the shots. It's what she always wanted and I was nothing without her. We argued, I left but I knew I couldn't keep Ramsay waiting for long. He's not a patient man and he makes his mind up on a whim. If he decides you're not worth the paper a contract is written on, he'll tear it up in front of you. So, I went back, back to Blanche's suite and there she was. Dead, murdered, lying on the bed, looking like the film star she's always been but cold and gone.'

Von Hiltz begins to sob again. You release your grip and ask why he didn't come forward when he was called by the staff at the reception desk. He apologises.

'I should have,' he said. 'But it's not easy for me. I have enemies here, in Hollywood, in America. There are people in this business who would relish the chance to have me put away, for crimes I haven't even committed. The studios for one. I cost them too much money, or so they claim. They don't complain when the box offices are bursting with dollars that my pictures have made them. But until that point, I'm public enemy number one. How do you think they would all react when they found out I was the one who discovered the great Blanche Aikerman dead? They'd have me strung from the nearest streetlight, or tossed me in the Pacific Ocean, without a second's thought. I'm not perfect, officer, not by a long stretch. But I work for my art and I'm not a killer.'

You look at the pistol lying on the floor. Von Hiltz clears his throat.

'Protection,' he says, sheepishly. 'I didn't dare run from this place, that would make me look even *more* guilty. Yes, I discovered Blanche's body, but I didn't put it in that room or slice her throat open like a pig. And if the killer was willing to rub out the most famous woman in the world, why wouldn't they do the same to me?'

Von Hiltz pushes the hair from his face. He straightens his tie and tucks his shirt back into his trousers, trying to tidy himself up.

'What are you going to do with me, officer?' he asks, a degree of trepidation in his voice. 'I'm innocent, innocent of murder at least. I would never have shot you, that was my mistake, I accept that. But with Blanche's murderer still out there, somewhere, you can understand my paranoia, surely?'

Without back-up, you've got two choices:

- You let von Hiltz go, warning him not to pull a stunt like this again and to remain in the building for future questioning

(turn the next page)

- You cuff von Hiltz and take him to the back entrance to meet Captain Barclay and the arriving LAPD (turn to page 81)

The director dusts himself off. He starts down the hallway but stops after only a few steps. Tapping his finger to his chin, he beckons you closer.

'You know, this whole situation has spiralled out of control,' he says. 'You'd think that being a director, an art maker like me, I'd have kept a lid on things much better.'

You're confused. He senses he's lost you and starts to laugh.

'Oh, come on, detective,' he says. 'You really think I'd be stupid enough to get caught like this?'

Before you can react, he darts his hand forward and grabs your pistol from the holster slung over your shoulder. You're still reeling when he pulls it free and fires. The hot kiss of the bullet thumps into your chest and you stagger backwards, gasping for breath. Your legs go from under you and you topple backwards, pain spreading out from the wound like tentacles, choking the life from you.

Von Hiltz appears above you, still laughing, your pistol smoking in his hands. He leans down and slaps you playfully on the cheek.

'You shouldn't be so trusting, officer,' he says. 'I'm sorry it had to be this way. But you see, there are certain things that need to stay secret. And having a cop, no matter how gullible, knowing too much is bad for business.'

He wipes the pistol handle clean on his shirt and drops it down beside you. He walks off down the hallway, laughing to himself. The world starts to turn a little darker and you realise now that this is the end.

While this may be the end of the case, you consider that letting von Hiltz go completely was perhaps a rookie mistake. With the sound of your old drill sergeants from the police academy ringing in your ears, you decide to place the director under arrest on the next page.

'But I'm innocent!' von Hiltz shouts. 'Didn't you hear a word I just said! I told you I didn't kill Blanche! I'll have your badge for this you flat-footed imbecile! I'm trying to help you!'

He proceeds to swear, a lot, in German. Thankfully there is nobody around and you're able to get him back down the stairs and out to the loading yard at the back of the hotel.

Captain Barclay is waiting with a small army of LAPD uniformed officers. When he sees you've handcuffed Peter von Hiltz, who is still shouting and swearing, his eyes go wide.

'What the hell are you doing?' the police captain cries.

You bundle von Hiltz down the steps of the loading bay and over to a waiting cruiser. You slam the door shut, instantly silencing the distressed director. Barclay pushes the rim of his fedora upwards, his fat face pink as a Christmas ham.

'This better be good,' he says. 'He's one of the most powerful men in Hollywood and you've just thrown him in the back of a cop car like a sack of potatoes.'

Von Hiltz is still angrily shouting in the car. You ignore him and take Captain Barclay aside. As you explain what's happened to Blanche Aikerman, that her body is still in the penthouse suite, and that von Hiltz pulled a gun on you, Barclay's face drains of the bright pink colour that you're familiar with.

'Holy cow,' he says, mopping his brow on the sleeve of his trench coat. 'This is big. This is *really* big. Blanche Aikerman, zotzed. Good god, we'll have a riot on our hands if this news gets out. And that's before the press start picking over her carcass. Do you have any suspects?'

You explain to Captain Barclay your theories. Nothing substantiated, nothing anywhere close enough to carry out an arrest or a charge. His face is turning a shade of grey at every turn of your progress.

'This is bad, this is *really* bad,' he says, looking about at the cops he's brought with him.

Then something changes in the captain's face. Like a lightbulb going off above his head, he turns to you, and speaks quietly.

'This could be history,' he says. 'Blanche Aikerman, the most famous actress in the history of Tinseltown, murdered. And just before her big night at the Golden Star Awards. We could be heroes, detective. You, me, everyone. We could be the heroes the newspapers and magazines talk about, like the sheriffs in the Old West. We have to play this carefully, by the book, but we need a collar, an arrest, *somebody* in custody.'

Slowly, he turns to look at von Hiltz in the back of the police cruiser. Barclay opens the door to a torrent of abuse. He grabs the director by the lapels, hauls him out of the back seat and slams him against the car.

'All right, Fritz, out with it,' he says, snarling. 'We know you found the body. Let's have your confession before I turn you over to the boys here.'

'Get out of my face!' von Hiltz rasps back. 'I don't deserve to be treated like this. I'm an American citizen!'

'Yeah, right. And I'm Donald Duck!' Barclay laughs. 'My detective here says you found Blanche and didn't report it. You want us to think you were innocent and just looking after yourself. Gimme a break!'

He slams von Hiltz into the car again. The director remains defiant.

'I told your *polizist*, I'm in fear for my life.'

'That's why you pulled a gun then? That's why you almost blew a hole in one of my officers' heads? Don't give me that Herr Traitor. I know what you lot are like, you can't be trusted.'

'This is abuse!' von Hiltz shouts. 'I know every lawyer in this town and they'll be foaming at the mouth to take a sleazeball like you, whoever you are, to court for the way you're treating me.'

'The only lawyer you're gonna see is the brief who tries to get you off of a murder charge. And believe me, Fritz, there's no jury in the land that won't want to see you fry in the chair for the murder of Blanche Aikerman.'

A collective gasp ripples around the gathered cops and coroner's office team. This is the first that any of them have heard that Blanche has been murdered. You feel the cold sweat gathering on the back of your neck.

The mention of the electric chair seems to snap von Hiltz's anger. His face immediately changes from one of rage to fear.

'Okay, all right, I know what this looks like,' he says. 'I shouldn't have pulled a pistol on your officer. But I'm innocent, you have to believe me.'

'They all say that,' says Barclay. 'Pity your apologies and your pleading didn't stop you from cutting that young girl's throat, isn't it?'

'I didn't do it!' von Hiltz screams.

'If you didn't do it. Then who did? Huh?'

The director looks at you. He gulps, panicking. He turns back to Barclay who is still holding him tight and up against the squad car.

'Elizabeth Gresham,' he says.

'The actress?' Barclay laughs. 'The living legend? Yesterday's leading lady? Get out of here.'

'They hated each other,' says von Hiltz. 'Gresham hates Blanche's success, her youth, her looks, everything. It all started when they were co-stars on that dreadful film, what was it, with the race around the world, I can't recall. Gresham was the star and Blanche was making her mark as an up-and-comer. You know what these actors are like. They'll do *anything* to stay in the limelight. She was here, Gresham, I saw her. I wouldn't put it past her to have taken her revenge on Blanche. She has nothing left to lose, she's box-office poison, hasn't worked in this town for years, she's at her lowest ebb.'

Barclay looks at you.

'Well?' he asks. 'What do you think?'

- With no clear evidence pointing to von Hiltz's guilt, you go against protocol and begin to think von Hiltz might be onto

something with Elizabeth Gresham on page 87

- Something about von Hiltz is making you question his innocence, so you decide to interrogate him further on the

next page

'I agree,' says Barclay. 'And I'm sure once the boys from the lab get a look at the crime scene, we'll find it swimming in evidence to back up our hunch.'

'You can't do this to me!' von Hiltz shouts as he's shoved back into the police cruiser. 'I'm innocent! I didn't kill Blanche Aikerman!'

Barclay slams the door closed. He puffs out his chest and looks around the backyard of the hotel.

'You did good work here, kid,' he says to you, clapping you on the shoulder. 'We've got a collar, a famous one at that. That should keep the press happy when I tell them about Miss Aikerman's murder. There might be a promotion in this for you. I'll have to have a word with the chief and the mayor.'

He smiles, leering, at you. Then he turns to the others who have all gathered around the squad car, hoping to catch a glimpse of the now disgraced Peter von Hiltz. They stare at him, like a caged animal at the zoo.

'All right, listen up,' he says. 'I don't know how much you know, but here's the situation. Blanche Aikerman, darling of the silver screen, has been murdered. The director Peter von Hiltz, who you can see behind me here, is the number one suspect. He resisted arrest, pulled a piece on one of our own, and is insisting on his innocence. And … he's German. That sounds about as guilty as you can get in my book. Now I need you to secure the crime scene and not let anyone in or out on my command. This is a big one, boys, a *huge* deal. You're going to be asked a lot of questions from the vultures in the press. Hold firm, don't say a word, it's not our jobs to make their lives easier. Any and every question and request comes to me. Is that understood?'

The gathered officers all nod in agreement.

'I want this to be a shining example of how good the LAPD really is, especially our world-class homicide department. We have a chance to make history here, boys. We'll be on the front cover of magazines, I … we might even get our own movies, who knows.'

A sense of excitement sweeps through the group. You watch as Captain Barclay laps up the adulation from his officers. He catches you staring at him and flips you a wicked wink. You look back at Peter von Hiltz sitting in the squad car. The director looks downtrodden, defeated. He is sulking, eyes watery from tears. The faintest sense of doubt begins to creep into your head.

'All right, men. Let's get to it.' Barclay claps his hands together.

The officers immediately spring into action, filing into the hotel, followed by the lab team. You catch Captain Barclay before he joins them to voice your concerns.

'Now listen to me!'

He grabs you by the lapels of your coat and slams you into the squad car. He looks around the yard to make sure there is nobody about. Then he speaks low, with a menacing sneer on his face.

'We've got this wrapped up nice and tight, you understand?' he says, breath hot on your face. 'Von Hiltz will hang for this, I'll see to it that he does. The press will have their villain and Blanche Aikerman will live forever – she'll be known as the martyr of Hollywood. A fitting end and legacy to one of our great American heroes, don't you agree?'

You don't get a chance to answer.

'This is tied up, open-and-shut case,' he says, threateningly. 'You'll get your chance to shine when the commissioner and mayor want to shake your hand. But this all ends here, right now, with that Fritz von Hiltz in custody and Blanche Aikerman given a proper send-off. I don't need some cavalier have-a-go hero cop working on their own to make things complicated. I don't need to tell you I can have your badge, just like that and you'll be flipping burgers on Sunset Boulevard faster than you can say Golden Star Awards.'

He snaps his fingers.

'Do I make myself clear, officer?'

Barclay releases his grip. He fixes his fedora, mops sweat from his top lip and winks at you.

'You did good, kid, real good,' he says. 'Now it's time for the professionals to take over. Keep your mouth shut, your thoughts to yourself and smile when I tell you to. That way we'll all be heroes before the day is out.'

He turns and stalks off towards the inner workings of the hotel. You're left alone in the back courtyard, surrounded by the police cruisers and squad cars. You look down at the nearest one and see Peter von Hiltz staring back at you. He is a broken man, ashen white, aged a hundred years in the last few moments since he was arrested by Barclay. You realise then that your career is at a crossroads. And you must decide which path you take, knowing all too well that whatever you *do* decide may affect not only this case, but your life as a whole.

You walk away, doing as you're told by Captain Barclay.
The case ends here for you. But you can always return to the
previous choice on page 83.

You placate Barclay, telling him what you think he wants to hear. The smug police captain nods and signals to the others to clear out. When the loading area is empty, you open the cruiser door.

'What are you doing?' asks von Hiltz.

You pull him from the cruiser and barge him across the loading square towards the alleyway that runs behind the hotel. You make sure nobody sees you as you've just released a prisoner from custody. This would be your badge if you were caught. But you're convinced that von Hiltz isn't the guilty party.

'I told you, I'm innocent, I wouldn't murder Blanche, why would I? Now that she's dead I'm not going to get my money from Ramsay and Thundersaga Pictures.'

You release his cuffs. He rubs his wrists.

'Your captain isn't going to be very pleased,' says the director. 'In fact, I imagine he'll see you swing too if this gets back to him.'

You assure von Hiltz that you know the risks. And that you're convinced that he isn't a murderer, at least, not of Blanche Aikerman.

'I'm not,' he says. 'And that means the killer is still running around here, somewhere. It could be anybody, Blanche wasn't exactly the easiest star to work with. The more her reputation grew, the more of a diva she became. She came from nothing, as I'm sure you know by now. And she was treated like dirt for the early parts of her career. I don't blame her for being bitter, the way some of these young actors and models are treated is abysmal. It's a tale as old as time, unfortunately. Only this time, Blanche has paid dearly with her life.'

Shouting drifts down the alleyway. The others have discovered that von Hiltz has gone. The director looks panicked as he turns to you.

'We have to go,' he says. 'I wasn't just trying to shift the blame to your captain. I really do think that Elizabeth Gresham may have had something to do with this. In fact, now that I think about it, I'm sure I saw her talking to Blanche earlier this morning. Yes, I'm sure I did, in the hotel lobby. She's a manipulative, conniving *arschgeige* if there ever has been one. I swore I'd never work with her again after the debacle of that western we had to abandon a decade ago. And she can't act, which is the worst part. If Blanche

Aikerman has been murdered by anyone in this town, Elizabeth Gresham had something to do with it.'

The shouting is getting louder. It won't be long before you're discovered by the other cops. You ask where Gresham may be.

'She was here earlier,' says von Hiltz. 'Swanning around like the Queen of Sheba. I swear, the only thing greater than her sense of impenetrable fame is her delusion. It would be hilarious if it wasn't so tragic. She's a joke in this town and has been for years. Yet she thinks she's the star of the show.'

You ask where von Hiltz last saw Gresham in the hotel. He shakes his head.

'She won't be here now, I know that much,' he says. 'The old boot is a recluse at heart. She'll have been here to show her wrinkled face and then straight back to that fortress she calls a home in Bel Air. Like a snake, slithering back to its lair, waiting on the pool boys or the mailman to come around so she can pounce. No, Elizabeth Gresham will be tucked up safely behind the cast-iron gates and ten-foot-high hedges of her lair by now.'

What do you think?

- You ask von Hiltz if he's just trying to deflect blame from himself in the following section

- You insist that von Hiltz takes you to Elizabeth Gresham's mansion (turn to page 92)

'Of course I'm not!' he shouts loudly. 'I've told you and that ape of a captain of yours, I didn't murder Blanche Aikerman. I had no reason to. No cause. If anything, I'm losing out on her being dead, with that contract up in smoke without her. Trust me, officer, there is nobody on this earth who had more to lose than I did with Blanche's murder. Except, perhaps, her mother. Although I've never quite believed that old prune's dying-swan act. She's a lot smarter than everyone in this business gives her credit for. The fact that the whole of Hollywood knows who Mrs Aikerman *is* is testament to that fact. You don't just wake up with a reputation in Tinseltown, officer, believe me. You have to earn it. And Mrs Aikerman is somebody who has earned her reputation, rightly or wrongly.'

'Hey!'

A voice echoes down the alleyway. Two uniformed LAPD officers have spotted you and von Hiltz. They draw their guns and command you to stand still. Von Hiltz is the first to run. He grabs you by the arm and you both take off down the dingy back street.

The crack of pistol fire echoes about you. Von Hiltz drops to the ground, struck in the back. As you stop and turn to get him, you feel the stinging bite of lead as a bullet tears into your chest. It sends you spinning and you land hard on the ground. The world seems fuzzy for a moment as you feel blood seeping from the wound in your chest. You realise then that your heart has been struck and you are moments from death. The last thing you hear is the approaching footsteps of the officers who gunned you down.

You have been killed for disobeying orders. Return to page 88 to try a different tactic with von Hiltz.

Quietly, you ease von Hiltz down the alleyway and into the street beyond. Looking behind you, nobody appears to have followed you. The sidewalk is busy, the glowing evening sun making everything seem that little bit warmer. But this is Los Angeles, and you know that there's nowhere colder on earth, especially when there's been a murder.

Keeping calm, you gradually make your way back around to the main entrance of the Royale Premiere. Unbelievably, the long driveway that leads to the main doors is busier than it was before. Valets are scuttling around trying to deal with the cabs, limousines and other vehicles all making their way in and out of the hotel grounds. You spot your car, still sitting where you left it earlier. Using the distraction of how busy things are, you and von Hiltz race to the motor and climb in.

'We're going to Bel Air, just north of the Country Club. It won't take us long,' says the director.

As you pull out of the driveway, a large laundry truck cuts in front of you. Your car screeches to a halt and von Hiltz almost hits his head on the dashboard. The truck driver stops chomping on his stogie long enough to shout obscenities at you. As you're about to pull away, there's a tap at the window.

'Are you all right?' asks a young LAPD officer.

It takes him a moment to realise who you are and, more importantly, who is sitting in the seat beside you.

'Hey!' says the young cop. 'Aren't you—'

Before he can say anything else, you hammer the accelerator. The car's engine roars into life and you fly forward, barrelling over the curb and onto the road.

'Good god!' von Hiltz pants, bouncing around in the seat beside you. 'Have you lost your mind?'

You check in the rear-view mirror. As the Royale Premiere retreats into the distance, the chilling sight of squad cars pouring out of the main entrance way makes your blood run cold. Von Hiltz turns around and looks out the back window.

'*Scheiße*,' he says. 'What are we going to do now?'

- You hit the gas and try to lose the police in the busy LA traffic on page 95 ⭐
- You pull over and hope you can reason with the officers pursuing on the next page ⭐

Realising that you can't outrun the might of your colleagues, you slow down and pull in at the side of the road.

'What are you doing?' von Hiltz exclaims. 'If they catch us, we're finished!'

You tell him you know that. You switch off the engine as the car is surrounded by cruisers. All of the officers, some of them you know, get out and train their guns and weapons on your car. They urge you to get out, slowly, with your hands in the air.

'If we set foot outside this car, we are done for,' says von Hiltz. 'They'll have me convicted before we reach any station. And you'll be an accessory. It's game over if we go out there.'

You nod solemnly, knowing the consequences of what you've done. Slowly, you climb out of the car. The officers are on you immediately and put you in cuffs. They do the same to von Hiltz who is swearing, once again, in German.

As the police lead you away to a waiting cruiser, you try to explain to them that you think von Hiltz is guilty. And that you were just following up a potential other subject. The officers aren't interested. They congratulate themselves on apprehending you and von Hiltz before you were able to make good your escape.

The cruiser door is slammed firmly shut on you. Handcuffed and alone, you watch through the window as von Hiltz is taken away into another police vehicle. Before he vanishes forever, he spots you and sneers. Drawing a line across his throat, he sends a chilling, silent message to you about your future.

Realising the trouble you are now in, it becomes clear that you've missed something along the way of the investigation. Why don't you see what Victor Ramsay is doing by turning back to page 58.

The other cars on the road whizz past you like mosquitos. It takes all of your concentration not to crash. A collision at this speed would surely be lights out for everybody involved.

A small fleet of police cruisers is following you. Their bright red lights and screeching sirens take up all of the rear-view mirror. They're gaining on you, the other traffic moving out of the way for them. It's for the best. They'd just run over anyone or anything that got in their path.

'Faster!' von Hiltz urges you. He's nervously slamming his fists into the dashboard. 'If they catch us, we're finished. Our feet won't hit the ground. They'll strap us to the electric chair tonight. Both of us. You're an accessory now.'

You didn't need reminding. But it serves as extra motivation to lose your colleagues now giving chase. The road signs are flashing by almost as quickly as the rest of the traffic. You've got no idea where you are – Bel Air, Beverly Hills, it could be Brooklyn for all you know. All that matters is to get away from the convoy of police cars now breathing down your neck.

'We have to lose them,' says von Hiltz. 'Can't you do something? Don't you police learn how to drive like maniacs at your academy.'

His commentary isn't helping. But something pops into your mind that might be of some use. Hurling the car around a corner, you race through a crossroads on the red light. Horns honk and tyres screech as the civilians try their best to avoid a terrible crash.

'They're gaining on us,' says von Hiltz.

No sooner has he spoken than a bullet pings off the side mirror. Another zooms overhead and a third shatters the back window of your car. You weave and stray across the road, narrowly avoiding an oncoming lorry.

Then your worst fears come true. A fork in the road up ahead. In all the excitement and terror, you've lost track of where you are in the city. But you've got a choice to make. One road or the other, it could be the difference between going to jail and solving this case.

- Left (turn to page 97)
- Right (turn to page 98)

'I hope you know where you're going,' says von Hiltz.

You take the left avenue, trying desperately to work out where you are in the city. But you don't have time. As the wailing sirens get louder from behind, you spot something dreadful up ahead.

'What's that?' von Hiltz shouts.

Ahead, the road is blocked by an overturned tanker. You hit the brakes, but the road is slick. The car slips and slides as you try to wrestle the steering wheel back in place. It's no use. Your car spins out of control on the road, von Hiltz screaming beside you. The jackknifed tanker rears up ahead and the distinct smell of diesel drifts into the cab.

Your car smashes into the tanker. There's a brief, still moment before a spark ignites the fuel spilling from the overturned lorry. Then everything goes up.

The case ends here for you. But you can always try heading right to get away from the LAPD on the next page.

'I hope you know where you're going,' says von Hiltz.

You don't answer him. The truth is, you're not wholly sure where you're going. Only that a convoy of the LAPD's finest boys in blue are hot on your tail. You take the right avenue and hit the gas. The traffic is beginning to ease up and it's not so hard to get across lanes. While it makes things a little easier, it also means the police can catch up faster. You just concentrate on the road and hope something presents itself.

'We're coming through Bel Air,' says von Hiltz. 'I know this place.'

Slowly the built-up mass of downtown Los Angeles retreats. Even the lavish houses and homes are dispersed by woodland and high, rolling hills.

'They're building one of your American freeways through here,' says von Hiltz. 'It should make the traffic a bit better in this godawful town.'

You don't need a lesson on civics and planning. Not right now. You weave your way along a narrow road as the woodlands slowly give way to the flats and more housing in the north of the city. The cops are still behind you, gathering pace and numbers. You realise then that it's going to take something drastic.

Somewhere in the back of your mind, you remember the area and this part of the city. Everything is expanding here in LA. It always is. For a city that's steeped in history and fame, it moves faster to create something new than anywhere else in the country. And that something new might just be your ticket out of here.

Hurtling the car around a corner, von Hiltz slams into the door.

'Do you want to tell me when you're going to do something like that!' he exclaims, rubbing his shoulder.

The road seems vaguely familiar and then you spot it up ahead. There's an overpass and, beyond that, your only chance to lose your colleagues. It's now or never. A quick, final glance at the rear-view mirror shows the LAPD getting closer and closer. This is it. Von Hiltz seems to have worked out what you're planning.

'No,' he says, grabbing hold of the dashboard. 'You can't, you can't possibly think this is going to—'

Before he can finish, you smash the car through the barrier of the overpass. For a brief moment, everything goes silent as the world slows down to almost a crawl. You can see for miles as the car glides effortlessly through the void. The brick and masonry that's just exploded on the hood of the car twists and turns like elegant ballerinas from the Bolshoi. Then the nose dips and you see your landing spot. You brace for impact. This one is going to hurt.

With a bang that rips through the whole cabin, you're down. The engine is still roaring and the wheels take grip on the man-made concrete of Bull Creek – a huge, artificial flood channel that bores its way through the northern part of the city.

You grip the steering wheel tight, so tight that your knuckles hurt. As you speed off down the flood channel, you catch sight of your colleagues skidding to a halt at the huge hole you've left in the overpass barrier. They are, quite sensibly, not following you. Von Hiltz only now opens his eyes, his teeth locked together, tendons flexing in his jaw.

He looks about, firstly at the flood channel speeding by, and then out of the back window. When he sees that the LAPD aren't following, he lets out a holler.

'You're mad!' he shouts. 'I don't know whether to kiss you or strangle you for taking such a terrible risk!'

You urge him to calm down as you put your foot down to get away from the cops as quickly as possible. The channel carries on for another mile or two before you take one of the old construction ramps that leads back to the main street level. Checking to make sure there are no patrols about, you round the car and start the journey back towards Bel Air and Elizabeth Gresham's mansion.

By the time you reach the affluent neighbourhood, the sun is little more than a thin, blood-red slice on the horizon. The streetlights are just blinking on as you make your way through the East Gate at Beverly Glen and Sunset Boulevard.

'Nothing is exclusive in Los Angeles anymore,' says von Hiltz.

He nods out the window at the construction sites along the road. More and more houses and mansions are being built here.

'The more money, the less special it all becomes,' he says bitterly. 'Lady Gresham has the right idea. Build your castle and hide in it for as long as possible.'

He points out the windscreen at a house on the end of a long boulevard. Thick hedges reach up from the sidewalk, broken only by a cast-iron gate that's firmly closed.

'Let me do the talking,' says the director. 'If she knows you're the police we'll never get in.'

You pull over to the side of the road and you both get out. Beyond the gates you can see the Gresham mansion. It's tatty and old-looking and needs a lick of paint. Von Hiltz pushes the gate and it creaks open with a painful groan.

Marching up the main path to the house, you reach the front door. It's nothing impressive, although you can tell that the land the mansion sits on is worth more than you could ever spend in a lifetime. Von Hiltz rings the bell and, after a few moments, the door opens just a little. A brilliant blue eye, surrounded by thick make-up that would make Cleopatra blush, appears on the other side.

'Who's there,' croaks an old voice.

'Elizabeth, it's me, Peter,' says von Hiltz.

The reclusive Elizabeth Gresham measures the both of you up for a moment from the safety of the crack in the door. You can almost hear the gears and cogs whirring around inside her head. When her calculations are complete, she opens the door wide and, with the biggest, fakest smile, she throws her arms out wide to greet the director.

'Peter, darling!' she says, kissing the air on either side of his head as she embraces him. 'What are you doing here? I thought you'd be at the Royale Premiere ahead of the big show tomorrow night.'

'Can we come in?' asks the director.

'Of course, come in, come in, can I get you a drink? The staff have gone home for the evening, but I can still fix you something that cooks. Nobody makes a Manhattan like Elizabeth Gresham, but I don't need to tell *you* that, do I, darling?'

The ageing Hollywood star leads you through her crumbling mansion, like a ghost gliding through the mist of a cemetery. Her gown is glittering and trails along the filthy floor like a tail. Her hair is thinning and obviously dyed. Her shoulders are rounded and her posture dreadful. This, you suspect, is the price of fame in Tinseltown for three decades or more.

Most of the furniture is old and tatty. Paintings hang on the walls, although dust sheets cover them up. You're led into a small snug that overlooks the garden, books and scripts are scattered across the floor and a musky smell of stale air fills the place.

Gresham heads for the small bar close to the patio doors, fingermarks and grime staining the glass. She begins mixing cocktails and, casually, throws over her shoulder.

'And to what do I owe the pleasure of two callers at this time of night?' she asks.

- Keep your cards close to your chest on the next page

- Tell Gresham about the untimely demise of Blanche Aikerman

on page 106

Gresham mixes you all drinks. She hands you something exotic looking in a fine glass and retires to a long couch in the far end of the room. Peter von Hiltz is sipping his own drink and casually strolls around the perimeter of the den. He's admiring the photographs that hang from the walls – black-and-white stills that show Gresham as a much younger woman, cavorting, dancing, schmoozing with the great and good of Hollywood's yesteryear.

'Now tell me, ' she says, 'you weren't brought here by Peter von Hiltz because you're my number one fan. Were you?'

You place your drink down on one of the nearby tables. You're on duty, after all. Elizabeth Gresham produces a sterling silver cigarette case. She takes out a cigarette and sparks it into life using a lighter that is probably worth more than you make in a year. The smoke snakes around in front of her face but she is still staring at you. Always staring.

'So, come on then,' she says. 'What's this all about?'

You don't want to spill too much information. If Peter von Hiltz is right and there had been some conflict between Gresham and the late Blanche Aikerman, you don't want to reveal too much to the ageing star. The director is still circling the room. He seems to pick up on your hesitance.

'Tell us, Elizabeth, my sweet,' he says, rounding on Gresham. 'What did you think of Blanche Aikerman?'

Gresham's face is stony and straight. The natural beauty that helped her conquer Hollywood is still there, somewhere, behind the thick layer of make-up and the lines of time. She doesn't shift her gaze from you at all. The smoke curls in front of her face before she takes a long drag from the cigarette.

'She is a talentless hack,' she says, flatly. 'The woman has about a tenth of my talent and none of my beauty. She's a rube, from the sticks, that managed to sleep her way to the very top of this industry. And I hope she rots in hell.'

Von Hiltz's eyebrows rise, wrinkling his forehead. He looks at you before draining his glass.

'You see,' he says to you. 'I told you they didn't get on.'

'What do you mean, we "didn't get on",' says Gresham. 'What's going on here? Peter? Why have you brought this police officer into my home? Am I under arrest or something?'

You decide that you should tell Gresham what's happened. When you do, a wry smile creeps across her face.

'So,' she says, sipping from her cocktail. 'Somebody caught up with that little bitch in the end. Can't say I'm wholly surprised. The amount of enemies she made in this town is too long, even for the roll call of Noah's Ark.'

Von Hiltz shrugs. He walks back around to be beside you.

'I told you,' he said.

'Told what?' asks Gresham. 'Peter? What are you talking about? You don't think I had something to do with this, do you?'

You tell Gresham that she was seen earlier speaking with Blanche before she was killed. You ask what the conversation was about.

'I wished her all the luck in the world,' says Gresham. 'She was all set to be crowned the queen of the universe tomorrow night. I know this sort of thing means a lot to young women like Blanche Aikerman. I tried to give her some advice, tried to bury the hatchet. We were never on the same page, too big a gap in our ages, I suppose. Among other things. But I warned her, I told her in no uncertain terms, that these awards, these gongs, these accolades, they mean nothing. When the applause has died and you're left on your own, you have to live with the consequences of your actions and decisions. I told her, pleaded with her, if you will, that she would not end up like me, a broken-down wreck living in a mausoleum of her faded memories. She didn't listen, of course. Why would she? Who am I to lecture the great Blanche Aikerman.'

Gresham reclines on the sofa. She pulls on the last of her cigarette before crushing it out into an ashtray beside her. She levels another of her calculated, cool, stoic looks at you.

'I didn't kill her,' she says. 'If that's what you're trying to surmise. Not that I didn't want to, of course. But, like I've said, officer, I didn't do it. Not only am I too old, I'm also dying.'

'What?' asks von Hiltz, baffled.

Gresham pushes a long strand of dyed hair from her face. She inclines her head towards a small cupboard in the corner of the room. Von Hiltz hurries over and pulls the door open. Two canisters fall out. He lifts a facemask and looks at the tanks.

'Oxygen,' he says, looking at Gresham.

'I'm afraid so,' she says. 'The doctors have given me six months to live. It would seem that my penchant for cocktails and fine cigarettes has caught up with me. And not a moment too soon. This town, this industry, it's nothing like it used to be. Far from it. Hatchet-faced prima donnas like Blanche Aikerman have turned it into America's trash heap. The whole world used to look to us for their entertainment. Now we can barely scrape together two cents to tickle the box offices. The sooner I'm gone, the better. I might make the headlines that way.'

'I don't believe it,' says von Hiltz, replacing the oxygen tanks in the cupboard.

'You had better believe it, darling,' laughs Gresham. 'Because I won't see Christmas. So, in answer to your questions, officer, yes, I did have motive and reason to kill Blanche. But I couldn't hurt a fly in this state, even if I wanted to. I am as weak as they come, that's why I spend all my time here, in the safety of my Xanadu. You may arrest me if you like but I'll never see the court.'

She holds out her wrists. Her hands are trembling and it's clear that she is a very sick woman. You shake your head. There is no need or reason to arrest Elizabeth Gresham. She is not the killer.

You turn to von Hiltz and say that you're leaving. As you prepare to show yourselves out, Gresham calls you back.

'You know, there is one strange part of all this,' she says. 'The fact that anyone got close enough to Blanche Aikerman to take her life. I mean, she's never alone, not with that meddlesome old hag Mrs Aikerman, her mother.'

'What do you mean?' asks the director.

'Honestly, she protected her better than the mob.'

'You're exaggerating,' laughs von Hiltz.

'Am I, Peter?' says Gresham. 'You're trying to tell me that Blanche's mother wasn't around her twenty-four hours a day, seven days a week? The woman was *always* there. I've even seen her on the red carpet at premieres, flanking Blanche like a shadow. I'm no detective. But if I was in your shoes, officer, the only person I'd be questioning about this murder is Mrs Aikerman. She never let her daughter out of her sight. And if that's the case, she'll know *exactly* who snuffed Blanche out.'

Intrigued by Gresham's take on Mrs Aikerman, you jump into your car and head to the hotel to speak with her. Turn to page 112 to follow this hunch.

The ageing Hollywood legend immediately drops her cocktail maker. The contents spill across the carpet, joining the other stains. Gresham does not react, her back still to you and von Hiltz.

'Murdered,' she says, voice barely louder than a whisper. 'Blanche Aikerman has been *murdered*.'

Slowly, she turns to face you both. Her face is like concrete, the wrinkles set, lips red and thin, like the cut on Blanche's throat. For a still moment, she just stands there, staring into the space between you all. Then something clicks in the back of her mind, and she remembers where she is and who she is talking to.

'Good, ' she says, turning back to the bar. 'That snotty-faced bitch deserves everything she gets. After what she did to me and countless others.'

'I told you they didn't get on,' whispers von Hiltz.

Gresham drains her glass. She shudders then composes herself. Filling another two, she hands them to you and von Hiltz before reclining on her sofa. She waves a hand around the room. Pictures hang from the walls, pictures of her as a young woman with some of the greatest stars of the day.

'This is all I have, now,' she says bitterly. 'Women like Blanche Aikerman have robbed me of my life, my income, my fame. They think all it takes to make it in this business is to flutter their eyelashes and wear clothes that don't fit. That's not what it is, that's not what acting is supposed to be. It's art. Do you understand? An art form, something that has to be managed and crafted, learned through experience and a life well lived. Not just parading about on stage like some hooker with a drug problem.'

'Very true,' nods von Hiltz, drinking down his cocktail.

'Don't make me laugh, Peter,' says Gresham, throwing her head back. 'You're just as bad as Aikerman.'

'What?

'You heard me,' she says. 'If it wasn't for flesh merchants like yourself, Hollywood would still be the great place it used to be twenty years ago. We'd still be doing something worthwhile, not the slap and giggle, cheap thrill pictures you and your studio buddies like to call cinema.'

'Now hold on a minute, Elizabeth, I—'

'Oh, save it for the rags,' Gresham cuts him off. 'I've read everything you've ever said, about the industry, about Hollywood.

You're a hack, Peter, a very good one. I'll give you that much. But a hack all the same. You couldn't direct a prestige picture if your life depended on it.'

That's enough to get Peter von Hiltz off his seat. He stamps his foot, like a petulant child.

'I don't need to stand for this,' he says. 'I'm a Golden Star winner, a fine director and artist. If I wasn't, do you think Thundersaga Pictures would be throwing money at me to stay with them?'

There's a venomous look in Elizabeth Gresham's eyes. She remains cool and calm, but fury is boiling away just behind her old Hollywood visage. You decide to step in and keep things focused. You ask Gresham where she was around the time of Blanche's murder.

'Here,' she says. 'I was at home. I'd had enough of that awful hotel and the people who make this town such a cesspit. Do you know that I was the box-office leading lady for ten years straight? I have more of those little trinket Golden Star Awards lying around this place than I know what to do with. And all of that meant nothing, absolutely nothing, when Blanche Aikerman and her cronies set foot on their first sets. Suddenly I was too "over the hill" to play the choice roles anymore. The directors, like your friend here, wanted fresh meat for the grinder. Sure, it started slowly, my agent wouldn't get calls about the major roles. Then it picked up steam, the only parts being offered were old aunts or grandmothers. Studios claimed that my attitude was what put directors and producers off, but I know it was, is, my age. Who wants to cast an old has-been from yesteryear when you've got these pretty little things running around town wearing their bathing suits and nothing else. No, I'm sorry to hear that Blanche has been murdered. No parent should outlive their child. But she had it coming.'

You ask about the conversation Gresham had with Blanche, the one that von Hiltz saw earlier that day.

'What did we talk about? I don't think that's of your concern, officer,' she says.

You press her.

'I wished her all the luck in the world,' says Gresham. 'She was all set to be crowned the queen of the universe tomorrow night. I know this sort of thing means a lot to young women like

Blanche Aikerman. I tried to give her some advice, tried to bury the hatchet. We never saw eye-to-eye, too big a gap in our ages, I suppose. But I warned her, I told her in no uncertain terms, that these awards, these gongs, these accolades, they mean nothing. When the applause has died and you're left on your own, you have to live with the consequences of your actions and decisions. I told her, pleaded with her if you will, that she not end up like me, a broken-down wreck living in a mausoleum of her faded memories. She didn't listen, of course. Why would she? Who am I to lecture the great Blanche Aikerman.'

Peter gives you a glance, like he's trying to tell you he was right. You're not convinced this is any sort of confession. And there is no evidence linking Gresham to Blanche's murder. Intent and motive is only part of the picture. You decide to out-and-out ask the old Hollywood star if she had anything to do with the killing.

'Please, officer,' she says, producing a sterling silver cigarette case and flipping it open. 'What do you take me for? If I had the heart to kill somebody, half of this town would be on a slab in the morgue. No, believe me when I tell you, nobody has been more wronged than me. Nobody. But that's no reason to go about bumping people off, now, is it?'

She sparks the cigarette with a lighter that's probably worth more than your annual salary. The smoke billows about her heavily made-up face as she stares at you from across the room. There's an alluring quality to her, despite the unequivocal rage that's simmering beneath the surface. You hold your gaze but can feel the heat of her hatred and bitterness permeating across the room.

'Even if I wanted to, I wouldn't ever get close enough to Blanche Aikerman to lay a finger on her,' says Gresham, tapping ash into a nearby ashtray.

'What do you mean?' asks von Hiltz.

'Mrs Aikerman,' says Gresham, sucking hard on her cigarette. 'That meddlesome old hag was always fussing around her daughter. Honestly, she protected her better than the mob.'

'You're exaggerating,' laughs von Hiltz.

'Am I, Peter?' says Gresham. 'You're trying to tell me that Blanche's mother wasn't around her twenty-four hours a day, seven days a week? The woman was *always* there. I've even seen her on the red carpet at premieres, flanking Blanche like a shadow. She was forever fussing, making sure everything was right with her beloved daughter. No hair was out of place, no crease in her frocks, no stray eyelash to ruin a photo opportunity. I'm no detective. But if I was in your shoes, officer, the only person I'd be questioning about this murder is Mrs Aikerman. She never let her daughter out of her sight. And if that's the case, she'll know *exactly* who snuffed Blanche out.'

- Intrigued by Gresham's take on Mrs Aikerman, you jump into your car and head to the hotel to speak with her. Turn to

  page 112 to follow this hunch

- Convinced that Gresham is hiding something, you press her for

  more information on the next page

'You'll have to forgive me, officer,' she says, stubbing her cigarette out and rubbing her temples. 'It's been rather a long day and I think I'll retire.'

She offers her hand into the air between you all. Peter von Hiltz immediately springs to action and takes it, helping the ageing actress up to her feet. She leads you both out of the den and back towards the main doors of the dusty old mansion. You thank her for her cooperation in the case.

'A pleasure,' she says, offering up her hand again for you. 'It's a dreadful tragedy and circumstance that things had to end this way. But, such is life, or at least it is here in Hollywood. I'm sure they'll make a great movie about your life one day.'

Her words linger for a moment. You think quickly, trying to work out if you heard her correctly. But before you can clarify, a hard thud on the back of your head sends you falling face-first into the floor. Your jaw cracks off the hard marble and you're immediately disoriented. You hear footsteps clicking around you and somebody rummages around in your pocket, pulling your pistol free.

As your vision clears, you feel the hot, sticky sensation of blood running down the back of your neck. You try to move but your legs are numb as Peter von Hiltz and Elizabeth Gresham loom over you. The director has a pistol trained on you and he's smiling.

'You shouldn't have been so trusting, officer,' he says. 'While your captain had the wrong reasons, he was absolutely right about me. Blanche Aikerman was nothing but a spoiled brat and somebody had to do something about her.'

'That's where I came in,' laughs Gresham. 'You see, dear Peter and I believe that cinema should and could be much better than the trash that Blanche Aikerman made. Yes, she'll die a martyr, but the thing about martyrs is, they can't make any more movies. Whereas I'm about ready for my great comeback, wouldn't you say so, dear Peter?'

'Absolutely,' says von Hiltz.

The two kiss passionately before he turns back towards you, your own pistol trained once more on your head.

'I'm afraid this is where your investigation ends, officer,' he says. 'I'll happily hand myself back into the police and tell them how you had murderous ambitions of fitting up my beloved Elizabeth

Gresham here. As for me, well, I had caught you in the process of trying to cover up your own murder of Blanche Aikerman, that's why I had to pull a gun on you back in the hotel. You're not the hero in this story, I'm afraid. Quite the opposite in fact. I'm sorry. Goodnight, officer.'

He pulls the trigger and you are shot between the eyes. Trusting von Hiltz and Gresham was a mistake. They were convincing, convincing enough to dupe a detective of your calibre. But your mistake has been costly. Perhaps returning to the hotel on the next page will yield less deadly answers.

Night has fallen on the City of Angels. Los Angeles always takes on a different quality when the sun has gone down. The streetlights glow, adding a magical aura to the whole city. At least, that's what the tourists think of it all. They walk around, hoping that they'll stumble across their favourite stars on the Sunset Strip just around the corner.

Even on the best days, that will never happen. You know better. You pounded these streets as a uniformed officer, fresh out of the academy. The only thing tourists might be surprised by is a mugger, ready to steal their purse and wallet, usually at gun point. Don't try to scream or run away, there are just more around the next turn.

There are no stars out tonight. They're all holed up in their rooms at the Royale Premiere. Tomorrow is the Golden Star Awards. And by now, you're sure that news of Blanche Aikerman's murder has reached every news desk, every hack, every hanger-on in this town, if not the whole world. And there will be a warrant out for von Hiltz's arrest. Yours too, probably. Returning to the hotel is a risk, but it's a calculated one.

Something that Gresham said to you has been ticking away in the back of your mind. The idea that Mrs Aikerman was never away from Blanche's side is hardly surprising. But the attention to detail, the almost obsessive lengths she apparently went to to keep her daughter the image of perfection, has sparked an idea in your mind.

Blanche's suite was immaculately tidy when you inspected it. No sign of a struggle, no sign of conflict. That contradicts what Peter von Hiltz has said about the actress, and the state of things when he last saw her alive. You conclude that the killer must have cleaned things over in the suite. And who would be most likely to do something like that than a doting mother?

If Elizabeth Gresham's suspicions about Mrs Aikerman are right, you need to question the victim's mother in a new light.

'What's your plan?' asks von Hiltz. 'Because I don't really feel like showing my face around that hotel if your colleagues in blue are all itchy with their trigger fingers.'

You don't have a plan. Not one that you want to share with the infuriating director anyway. He senses you're holding something back.

'You can just let me out here,' he says, pointing at the nearest street corner. 'I can hitchhike my way back to Düsseldorf. It's safer than the Royale Premiere, that's for sure.'

You ignore von Hiltz. Driving through the night-time streets of LA you spot the huge beams of light long before you see the hotel. Huge spotlights have been set up outside the Royale Premiere as festivities get underway for the biggest night in Hollywood's glittering calendar. Slowing to a stop a little further down the road, you gesture to von Hiltz to get out.

'You know you can't just waltz in through the front door,' he says. 'Your Captain Barclay will have made sure there are sentries on every door, nook and cranny.'

The director is right. Barclay will be eager to try and put you and von Hiltz under arrest. There will be a city-wide search ongoing, with border police and airports on standby. Your only hope is that you can sneak back into the hotel and get to Mrs Aikerman before the police catch you.

You urge von Hiltz down the street and duck down an alleyway. It runs along the back of the buildings and eventually leads back to the loading yard at the rear of the Royale Premiere.

'Back where it all began, huh?' von Hiltz smirks.

The LAPD cruisers are still parked up from earlier. There doesn't appear to be anyone standing guard and you both sneak across the yard and into the hotel. Being careful not to draw too much attention to yourselves, you make your way through the bowels and back passages of the Royale Premiere until you reach the staff entrance to the main lobby.

Peering through a gap in the door, the place outside is swarming with guests, journalists, hotel staff and police. It's busier than you've ever seen it. You whisper to von Hiltz that you should head to his room and use it as a base. He nods and you retreat back into the corridors and find a stairwell. It leads you up to the top floor, the level just beneath the penthouse suites. The place is quiet and tape has been placed over von Hiltz's room door. You ignore it and go in, closing the door behind you.

'Look at this place,' he sighs, staring at his belongings strewn across the floor. 'Your friends in the LAPD have been over this place with a fine tooth comb. Not that they'd find anything of course. I'm completely innocent. Still, this was a lovely room and private life I had, once.'

He shakes his head and makes a feeble attempt at cleaning up. Von Hiltz sits down on the bed and rubs his face, exhausted.

'This is not shaping up to be the exciting weekend I thought it was going to be,' he says. 'First Blanche Aikerman is murdered, then I escape from the police, chased by a fleet of the boys in blue, then Elizabeth Gresham tells me that the killer was right under our nose all along. And to top it all off, I've had my belongings rifled through like some common criminal. When will it end?'

You ignore him, moving over to his balcony doors. You slide them open and peer outside. The pool of the hotel is far below you, guests milling around at an extravagant pre-awards party. The twinkling lights of Hollywood and Los Angeles beyond that dot the horizon, bright against the inky blue darkness of the night. You look upwards and see there is another balcony above you. You ask von Hiltz about it.

'The penthouse suites,' he says. 'Blanche Aikerman's room is up there. And her mother's for that matter. Mrs Aikerman was staying in the suite beside Blanche, as she always does.'

You look up at the balcony above. Then down the dozen storeys below to where the party and pool deck are.

What do you do?

- To avoid being caught, you choose to climb up onto the balcony

  on the following page

- Feeling more secure with your feet on the ground, you head

  back out into the corridor on page 116

The banister that runs the width of the balcony isn't as strong as you first thought. As you clamber up, you feel the iron bars quivering beneath your shoes. Gripping onto the masonry of the balcony above, you try to get a proper handful. As you try to clamber up, the screws of the banister come loose from the walls.

You wobble, only slightly at first, then it gets worse. Suddenly you're tipping backwards with nothing between you and the pool terrace all the way below. You scramble, trying to hold on to the balcony upstairs but the masonry crumbles under your fingertips.

There's a brief, almost serene moment where everything slows down. You're weightless, watching the balcony, the penthouse suites above, the Royale Premiere atop the building all come into view. Then gravity and reality kick in, a double-barrelled blast that sends you reeling.

The drop is mercifully quick. The impact on the terrace below is brief but devastating. You don't feel a thing. Everything has turned dark.

Scrambling up the outside of hotels was a bad idea. Caught between a rock and a hard place, maybe taking your chances inside the hotel on the next page is a safer ploy.

'You'll be caught for sure,' says von Hiltz, urging you to stay. 'And if you get caught then it won't be long before they come after me, will it? I don't want to fry for this.'

You ignore the director and head for the door. Checking to make sure the corridor beyond is clear, you slip out and leave von Hiltz behind. Making your way down the hallway, you reach the stairs and climb them to the penthouse suite level. No sooner do you open the door when you hear a click from behind.

'Well, well, well,' says Captain Barclay, his revolver jamming into your back. 'Look who's decided to show their ugly face around the crime scene. Come back to inspect your handiwork, eh?'

You raise your hands as the captain ushers you into the main hallway of the penthouse floor. Two uniformed officers standing guard a little further up the corridor spot the captain and immediately rush over. They draw their weapons and pull your pistol from the inside of your trench coat.

'Let me see if I've got this straight,' says the captain as you're handcuffed. 'You directly disobey my orders, you help a suspected murderer escape, you lead your colleagues on a wild-goose chase across the city, risking their lives I might add, then you come back here to inspect the scene of the crime. Not looking very good for you, is it? One might even say you're an accessory to the murder of Blanche Aikerman. After all, you *were* here very quickly, before anyone else, in fact. Yes, I've always suspected you were no good, a trussed-up thug with a badge and a gun. Well, I'm telling you something now, dirt bag, I'll make sure you fry alongside that Kraut pal of yours. Take this piece of trash away, boys!'

The uniformed officers snap into action. They huckle you down the hallway. As you pass Blanche Aikerman's room, now completely sealed off by the lab techs, you see Mrs Aikerman inside. She's watching everything unfold in front of her. She spots you being led away by the police. A wry, twisted, knowing smile creeps over her face and she waves at you. You know, then and there, that Elizabeth Gresham was right all along. And that Mrs Aikerman has played a part in her daughter's death.

You reach the elevators. As you wait for the lift to arrive, you think of everything that's happened since you arrived at the Royale Premiere earlier this afternoon. Hard as it is to believe, it now looks like you're facing a spell in the Big House for helping von Hiltz escape and fleeing your colleagues. And a cop behind bars never ends well.

The elevator arrives. Two more uniforms are waiting for you inside. You step in, flanked by your now former colleagues. You realise then that as soon as the doors close, your life will be gone. And Mrs Aikerman will have succeeded, for whatever reason, in murdering her daughter.

What's your next move?

- Let the elevator doors close on page 129

- You leap out of the lift at the last second, escaping the police,

  on page 118

Shouts of protest chase you down the hallway as the doors close firmly shut behind you. None of the officers could react quickly enough and you've escaped them. You bolt down the hallway and reach Blanche Aikerman's room just as Captain Barclay spots you.

'Hey!' he shouts, pulling his gun again. 'Come back here!'

You barrel into the room, barging one of the tech boys out of the way. You head straight for Mrs Aikerman who is overseeing the whole forensic operation. When she spots you, her milky blue eyes go wide.

'Stop!' she shouts.

Blanche Aikerman's suite is crawling with more officers and the forensic team. You hurdle over a sofa and grab Mrs Aikerman by the shoulders. Spinning her around, you use the old lady as a shield as everyone trains their guns on you. Captain Barclay shambles into the room, face red as beetroot. When he sees you've taken Mrs Aikerman hostage, he snarls.

'Don't be stupid,' he says. 'You're in enough trouble as it is.'

You make sure that Mrs Aikerman is in front of you at all times. That way nobody will open fire. You demand the others all put away their guns and ask that you get the chance to speak.

'Do it,' barks Barclay. 'Put your weapons down. We don't want Mrs Aikerman being hit by a stray bullet from one of you morons!'

The assembled group of officers all look at each other. Then they slowly lower their pistols.

'All right,' says the captain. 'Now let's all just keep our heads here. Nobody has to get hurt. We just need to talk things through, that's all.'

It's strange to hear Barclay being diplomatic for a change. You had half expected him to come running into the suite, all guns blazing, like Wyatt Earp. Instead, he's relatively calm, despite his head being the colour of the red carpet downstairs.

'What do you want?' he asks.

You shift uneasily from one foot to the other.

'Who cares about that!' Mrs Aikerman screams. 'Just shoot! They're clearly mad! They'll kill me.'

You decide to roll the dice. There's little else left you can do in a situation like this. You accuse Mrs Aikerman of murdering Blanche. The room falls silent and Captain Barclay almost faints.

'What?' Mrs Aikerman gasps. 'How dare you. How very *dare* you say something like that to me. My daughter has been murdered. Killed in cold blood. And you think I had something to do with it?'

'What are you doing, you maniac?' Barclay shouts. 'Do you know how absurd that accusation is?'

'Yes, absurd!' says Mrs Aikerman.

You back yourself and Mrs Aikerman into the corner of the suite. You list off your suspicions to the gathered group. You mention that Mrs Aikerman has been constantly by the side of Blanche throughout the actress's rise to fame. That Peter von Hiltz discovered the body before anyone else. And how, working on timings and witness statements, there was no way anyone could access, murder and escape Blanche's suite without being close. So close, in fact, that only Mrs Aikerman's room next door would be able to offer that kind of swift in-and-out access.

The room is silent. All eyes are on you and Mrs Aikerman. The old woman is breathing heavily as you hold her tight. Then she begins to laugh.

'You're a clever one,' she says, tossing a dismissive look over her shoulder. 'A lot smarter than you look.'

'What?' gasps Captain Barclay. 'What are you trying to say, Mrs Aikerman.'

'Oh, shut up, you imbecile,' says the old lady, pulling herself free from your grip. 'Honestly, I've never met a man talk so much and do so little in my entire life. And I've lived through two world wars and countless presidents.'

She walks a little away from you. All eyes are on her now, every cop, Captain Barclay, even you, staring at Mrs Aikerman to see what she'll do next. The old woman is enjoying every minute of the attention. She stops at a table by the sofas of the penthouse suite. A large bouquet of roses sits in a priceless vase on the tabletop. Stopping to sniff the petals, she smiles and turns back to you.

'I always wanted to be a star,' she says. 'Acting, dancing, comedy, tragedy. I wanted to do it all. I'd have done *anything* to see my name in lights. Broadway, the West End, when it was all a game for gentlemen and ladies. Not like now. It's a circus, you all have to understand that. A maddening, endless merry-go-round where everyone competes to be the top dog, the star. And my daughter had everything, absolutely *everything* it took to make her that star. What's more, she had me.'

Mrs Aikerman thumbs her own chest. Everyone in the suite is silent, hanging on her every word.

'I know what people say about me,' she says, plucking a single rose from the vase. 'They say I'm meddlesome, that I interfere too much. It doesn't take much to rub people up the wrong way in Hollywood, as I've found out at my peril. But it's been worth it, absolutely worth every drop of sweat, every tear, to make sure my Blanche was the superstar, the icon, that she became. Or will become, now that she's dead.'

'I don't understand,' says Captain Barclay, rubbing the back of his head with the handle of his revolver. 'Are you trying to tell me that this is all *true*? That *you* murdered your own daughter?'

Everyone, including you, looks to Mrs Aikerman again for a response. She circles the suite, moving between the gathered officers like a ghost. She wistfully sniffs at the rose she's taken from the bouquet. When she reaches the doorway to the room where Blanche was murdered, she stops. Gazing at the blood-soaked bed, Blanche's body long removed, she smiles a little.

'Immortality and legend are terms that are thrown around far too often these days,' she says. 'Especially here in Tinseltown. Everyone is a legend as soon as they score their first box-office hit. Or they get a number one record. It used to mean something, it used to be a moniker that was hard earned through achievement, style, grace, class. Now you can be called an icon if you sweep up at The Brown Derby on a Saturday night, when the drunks and winos are tossed out. Blanche was better than that, she had the talent to make sure she could be a *genuine* legend in this industry. But talent isn't enough, not anymore. No, you need something else, something extra, that star quality that you can push over the top of the mountain, to set you apart from the rest of the bottom-feeders that call this city their home. Immortality, ladies and gentlemen, can only be achieved through tragedy. That's why she had to die.'

Mrs Aikerman carefully cups the rose petals in her hand. She turns back to face the room.

'I killed my only child,' she says, a single tear running down her wrinkly cheek. 'I took her life, slit her throat. She wasn't expecting it, why would she? I was her mother, the one person in the whole world who was supposed to protect her. And protect her I did, from the monsters in the press, the leering creeps and perverts in the boardrooms and on the sets. I protected her from all of that, and for what, to make her immortal, to make her name synonymous with cinema and Hollywood and fame for the next hundred years. Nobody remembers washed-up hacks like Elizabeth Gresham. Why would they? They rot and waste away in dusty old houses until finally they meet their maker, penniless and without a second's thought. Die, be murdered even, in your twenties, and you'll live forever. Simple, really, when you think about it.'

'Good god,' says Barclay. 'I think I'm going to be sick.'

'I did her a favour,' says Mrs Aikerman, nodding and staring down at the rose in her hands. 'I made sure that she would always be remembered. Cutting her throat, on the eve of her greatest achievement, you couldn't write that script if you lived to be a thousand years old. And while Blanche will ascend to the pantheon of Hollywood gods, I'll bear the terrible brunt for my actions. After all, what kind of mother would I be if I didn't accept that responsibility?'

Mrs Aikerman closes her hands around the rose. The flower crumples and she drops the petals on the floor.

'There you have it,' she says, bowing a little. 'My confession, my limelight moment. Just wait until you read what they say about me in the papers.'

Despite her frail appearance and age, Mrs Aikerman snatches a pistol free from a nearby officer before he can do anything. She trains it on you. The assembled cops, including Captain Barclay, raise their weapons.

'Don't even think about it,' says your commanding officer. 'You move an inch and this whole room will blow you to hell before you can even think Golden Star Awards.'

Mrs Aikerman flinches. Her milky-blue eyes scan the room at the dozens of officers all aiming at her. Without another hesitation, she lifts her stolen pistol and jams the barrel under her chin.

How do you act?

- Quickly (turn to page 123)
- Immediately (turn to page 125)

MURDER IN TINSELTOWN

The bang deafens you and the others. Mrs Aikerman drops like a stone, dead before she hits the ground.

'Good god,' says Barclay, tipping the rim of his fedora skyward.

You both walk around the sofa and survey Mrs Aikerman's body. A large pool of blood is forming on the carpet around what remains of her head.

'What a terrible waste,' whistles the captain. 'Killed her own daughter just to get famous. I tell you, kid, this world is getting worse. It feels like every turn just makes everything that little bit madder.'

'Captain,' comes a voice from the bedroom.

You look up and see one of the lab technicians holding a bloody knife. The air-conditioning vent above the four-poster bed has its grille removed.

'Found it in there,' he says. 'We'll have to check but I'm guessing it's the murder weapon.'

'Yeah,' says Barclay, turning and heading for the door. 'Clean up this mess, would you? I'm going to go downstairs and tell the press that we have our culprit.'

He stops in the doorway. Turning, smiling, he nods.

'Good work on this, kid,' he says, then disappears down the hallway.

You're left standing in the middle of the penthouse suite as the controlled chaos of the police investigation unfolds all around you, almost like you're not there. Hard as it is to believe, Blanche Aikerman was alive and well in this room just a matter of hours before. Now she and her mother, her killer, are both dead. All while the world sits and waits, anxiously, to find out what will happen next. Thanks to your investigative skills and gut instinct, they'll know the truth. And yet, you can't help but still hear Mrs Aikerman's words ringing in your ears.

'My confession, my limelight moment. Just wait until you read what they say about me in the papers.'

Was she right all along?

The case ends here for you. But you can always start again by turning to Chapter 1.

You both tumble to the ground. The gun goes off, somewhere amongst the tangle of limbs. It's not killed you, that's a plus. It doesn't take much effort to disarm Mrs Aikerman. Suddenly you're both swamped by the other officers of the LAPD who have sprung into action.

They drag you free from Mrs Aikerman and haul her to her feet. She's snarling at you, at Captain Barclay, at the cops slapping the handcuffs on her bony wrists.

'You think this is the last you'll hear from me?' she cackles. 'I'm about to become the most famous person in the world! I'm the one who killed Blanche Aikerman. I created her, crafted her, built her up from nothing. And I'm the one who took her away from everyone, snatched her life, just like that, with a kitchen knife no less! I'll be the villain of all villains when this gets out. Can you imagine? I'll live forever now. I'm a god!'

'Get her out of here,' says Captain Barclay.

He thumbs towards the door and the officers do as they're told. Mrs Aikerman tries to resist but the uniforms are too strong for her. They drag her out of her daughter's penthouse suite, her laughing and screaming echoing down the hallway.

Barclay claps a meaty hand on your shoulder.

'I never knew you were such an athlete,' he says. 'The US team might fancy some of those long leaping skills at the Olympics in Rome in a few years' time.'

'Captain,' comes a voice from the bedroom.

You look up and see one of the lab technicians holding a bloody knife. The air-conditioning vent above the four-poster bed has its grille removed.

'Found it in there,' he says. 'We'll have to check but I'm guessing it's the murder weapon.'

'Yeah,' says Barclay. 'Hey. What's that?'

He points down at your stomach. Your shirt has turned scarlet as a large blot of blood soaks into the fabric. Only then do you realise you've been shot – Mrs Aikerman's gun must have struck you when it went off during the scuffle.

Your legs turn to jelly and you slump forward. Captain Barclay catches you before you fall to the ground.

'Easy, easy now,' he says, laying you down. 'Medic! Can we get a medic in here!'

The world is starting to go a little hazy. Then the darkness creeps into the edges of your vision. The last thing you see is Captain Barclay, his big, red face peering down at you. Then everything goes black.

～～～～～

The hospital food isn't up to much. But you try and eat something every time the nurses bring you a meal. If for nothing else it keeps them off your back.

You are recovering well from the bullet. The doctors say that you lost consciousness for around twelve hours and that gave them time to operate. You were incredibly lucky by all accounts. No major organs were damaged, although you lost a lot of blood. If the LAPD hadn't acted as quickly as they did, you might not be here.

The last few days have been something of a blur. Among the usual visitors, friends and family, Captain Barclay has been bringing you newspapers every morning before he heads to the squad room. He's also recommended you to the commissioner for some sort of medal, going above and beyond the call of duty. You won't hold your breath on that front. Captain Barclay has already become something of a minor celebrity for heading up the homicide unit that dealt with this case.

The news of Blanche Aikerman's murder, at the hands of her mother no less, has been front-page news all week. Special tributes were paid at the Golden Star Awards the evening after the tragedy. And Peter von Hiltz was honoured with a special lifetime achievement gong for his troubles.

While you remain in hospital, you realise, sadly, that everything Mrs Aikerman had hoped and dreamed of when she plotted to kill her daughter, has come true. The media has already vaulted Blanche Aikerman to untouchable status, with lengthy, tribute pieces running all day, every day on the radio. Fans have gathered outside the Royale Premiere, leaving flowers and candles and holding all-night vigils in her honour. The whole hotel has turned into something of a shrine to the late, great star.

There's even talk of a new, permanent memorial on Hollywood Boulevard to commemorate Blanche and other legends of stage and screen. Everything, it would seem, that Mrs Aikerman had predicted would happen. All of her doing, in the most tragic of ways. And none of this would have been possible without your investigative skills and gut instinct.

As you sit in your hospital bed, staring out at the brightness of another Los Angeles day, you can't help but still hear the killer's words ringing in your ears.

'My confession, my limelight moment. Just wait until you read what they say about me in the papers.'

Was she right all along?

The case ends here for you. But you can always start again by turning to Chapter 1.

The elevator descends to the lobby. When the doors open again, you're met with a flurry of flashbulbs as the press all descend on you and your escort. Questions are hurled at you as the uniformed officers lead you through the lobby and out to a waiting cruiser.

You're put in the back of the car, the door slammed firmly shut. The driver gets in, turns on the sirens and snakes his way through the crowd all flanking the cruiser. When you're clear of the hotel, you let out a sigh.

'Don't fancy your chances, buddy,' says the driver, laughing a little as he looks at you in the rear-view mirror. 'When the cons in San Quentin find out you were one of us, you're going to take the count, big time.'

He laughs louder now as he drives through the city.

The case ends here for you. But you can always start again by turning to Chapter 1.

You follow Carter the waiter down the hallway. Mrs Aikerman can be heard sobbing behind you, Mr Walter trying his best to console her. You know that he's facing an impossible task. The woman's daughter has just been murdered. And the wisecracking comments of Carter have thrown gasoline on the fire.

You catch up with the waiter as he's stepping into the elevator. The doors close and it's just the two of you.

'Celebrities, huh?' he shrugs at you. 'I bet you have to deal with these assholes all the time.'

You don't answer that.

'I've not been working here that long. But let me tell you, buddy, it's no walk in the park. You think waiting tables and fetching expensive champagne for the rich and famous will be a breeze. But it's the opposite. These guys, they live in a different world, on a different planet. They don't know how much gas costs, let alone what's going on out there in the city, the country. I'd quit if it wouldn't break my mom's heart. We're from Compton, the old Compton mind you. Not this shiny new suburb the city is so proud of. This job gives me career prospects, as my mom likes to tell me every five minutes. Otherwise I'd tell Walter where he could stick his head.'

The doors open. The cacophony of sound from the lobby washes over you like the Pacific. Carter marches out and hugs the wall, heading to the staff area behind the scenes. You follow him, wanting to question him about Blanche's body.

'Not exactly what you expect to see when you start your shift,' he laughs.

He has a relaxed manner, like nothing in the world would bother him. You'd think that was strange in any other case, especially after finding Blanche Aikerman's lifeless body in her bedroom. But Carter exudes a confidence, a salt-of-the earth sensibility. It's hard *not* to believe him.

'I brought her up her usual stuff and when nobody answered the door, I just let myself in,' he says as you push through a door and into the inner workings of the hotel.

The hallways and corridors are stark and bare here. There's a strong smell of cooking wafting down from the kitchens and staff hurry back and forth.

'She's just lying there, still. I called to her but she didn't answer. Then the closer I got, the more I realised that she'd been killed. The big cut on her throat was a dead giveaway, pardon the pun.'

You stifle a smile.

'So I hightailed it out of there and let Mr Walter know. He was his usual self, all self-importance and panic. I wonder how he sleeps at night knowing all the dirty dealings and goings on in this place. It's above my pay grade, thankfully. But the lives of celebrities, like Blanche Aikerman and her cohort, they're not for the faint-hearted.'

You ask Carter if he saw anyone else coming or going from Blanche's room. He shakes his head.

'It's pretty quiet up there, even at the best of times. The penthouse suites are like a whole other detached world, even from this place. The only other room up there is next door to the main suite. That's where Mrs Aikerman was staying. The old bag was just as demanding as her daughter. Seriously, I don't think Blanche could go for a piss without her mom knowing what she was doing.'

You thank Carter for his help.

'Sure, any time,' he says.

Carter is about to head up to the kitchens when he stops. He raises his hand and waggles his finger.

'There was one thing, though,' he says, turning back to you.

He looks about the hallway to make sure there is nobody about. Then he steps in closer to you, his voice low.

'Mr Walter,' he says. 'When I came back downstairs to tell him about what happened to Blanche Aikerman, he seemed a bit jittery, a bit odd.'

You ask in what way.

'Well, he was in his office for one thing, that was the first part that struck me as odd,' says Carter. 'I mean, for the manager of this place, he never sets foot in his office. He's always out schmoozing with guests or inspecting us regular Joes to make sure our shoes are shined or we don't count our tips in public. He's a real hard-ass when it comes to that sort of stuff. I think he enjoys it. Anyway, I came down to reception and the girls out front said he was in his office. I thought, "Hang on, Mr Walter, in there, on the busiest weekend of the year." That seems strange. And now that Blanche Aikerman has been killed, well, anything is possible, right? The most famous film star in the world dead, it makes you question everything you've ever thought about people and things. You must get that all the time in your line of work I guess.'

You ask Carter where Walter's office is.

'Just around the corner there,' he says, pointing down the corridor, past the kitchens. 'He's never in there, like I said. I don't even think he locks the door. Nothing to steal from a place that's hardly used, huh?'

You thank Carter for the information and let him return to his duties.

What's next?

- You head straight to Walter's office on page 135

- You head back to the front reception desk and ask the staff to

  put a call out for Mr Walter on page 134

The reception staff are happy to oblige. They send out a message for Mr Walter on the public address system. While you're waiting, you scan the lobby. The whole place seems much busier now than it did when you first arrived. Seeing the staff, the dignitaries, famous faces coming and going, you're suddenly hit with the weight of what has happened upstairs in the penthouse.

Keeping Blanche Aikerman's murder under wraps for as long as possible is key to conducting your investigation. The less people know about it, the greater surprise you have on your side. If the killer is still among the denizens of the Royale Premiere then you have to use every advantage you can to try and catch them – either before they escape or they strike again.

Ten minutes pass and there's no sign of Mr Walter. You ask the reception staff to put out another call for the hotel manager. You wait another five minutes. It appears that Mr Walter isn't showing.

Where to next officer?

- Walter's office on page 135?
- Back to the crime scene on page 48?

The door to the office was unlocked. You open the door with ease and step inside.

Walter's office is a cramped little space. Everything has a stagnant, unused quality to it. A chair on castors sits behind the desk, the leather unused and flat. Nothing like your trusty old seat back at the station. The desk is virtually clear, save for a few scattered folders. Filing cabinets line the walls, but they look almost brand new, untouched. On the far wall is a large painting. It's an original, you can tell right away, and shows the Royale Premiere at sunset. It's an impressive picture, you'll give Walter that. Although sitting at the desk having that thing bearing down on you can't be easy. You imagine Walter feels like he's constantly being watched by his bosses. He might well be in charge on the floor of the Royale Premiere – but there's always a bigger fish.

You inspect the filing cabinets first. They're unlocked and contain files. It appears to be employee records. You leaf through them until you find Carter's profile. His folder is almost flat, only one sheet of paper inside, with a picture of the waiter clipped to the top.

'Honest, hardworking, tends to shoot his mouth off. Not promotion material,' is written in an assessment box. Walter's signature is at the bottom of the page.

You put the file back in the drawer and close the cabinet. Next you try Walter's desk. There's not a lot to check out here. Most of the drawers are empty, not even a paper clip or a pencil to be seen. That is until you come to the very last drawer.

To your surprise, a switchblade rattles into view. Pulling out your handkerchief, you lift the weapon by the handle and place it down on the desk surface in front of you. Alarm bells are ringing in your head. Given Blanche Aikerman's throat was cut, any sign of a knife is enough to get the hairs on the back of your neck to stand on end. Carefully, you press the little button on the end of the handle. A four-inch blade flicks out. It's clean. No marks or blood on the glistening metal. You hold the knife up to the light. It looks like the blade has been recently cleaned – the faintest of rub marks streaked along the polished metal.

You wrap the weapon in your handkerchief and place it in the pocket of your coat. You don't want to get ahead of yourself. There are a hundred different reasons as to why Mr Walter would have a knife like this in the drawer of his seldom-used desk. It could have been planted there, or belong to somebody else. But you're not taking anything for granted. Never look a gift horse in the mouth, as your dear old gran used to say.

You check the drawer to make sure you haven't missed anything else. There's a folder lying flat on the bottom. You pull it out and a flurry of receipts drops out. Inside the file are statements and what look like bills. Bright red stamps with 'Overdue' and 'Insolvency' stand out immediately.

At a quick glance, it appears that bills are mounting in the running of the hotel. From suppliers invoices to empty accounts, a picture of a venue in deep trouble, or mismanagement, lies in front of you. You're about to inspect the documents more closely when something catches in your periphery.

'Oh!'

It's Mr Walter. The tall, slender, greying hotel manager is standing in the door of his office. He spots you, his eyes growing as large as dinner plates when he notices the drawer to his desk is open. Without a second's extra thought, he vanishes, taking off up the hallway.

Do you follow after Walter or look more closely at the documents in his office?

- You chase him on page 138

- You spend some time furthering your investigation into Walter

  on the next page

The fact that Walter has fled implies guilt. You won't have any problems putting out a call to find him. After all, there can't be too many middle-aged white men in formal dress looking flustered running around Los Angeles today.

You take a closer look at the documents in the file. The bills appear to be mounting up, some for Walter directly, others from suppliers of the Royale Premiere. It would appear that there's a lot of money flying around and the manager is at the centre of it all. Your mind ticks over. With the switchblade in the drawer and his odd behaviour after finding Blanche Aikerman, it's possible that Walter is a suspect in all of this. And if that's the case, you're going to need back-up.

You tidy up the files and tuck them into your coat pocket. Closing the door of the office behind you, you make your way back out to the main lobby and the reception. Before you plot your next move, the friendly receptionist from earlier waves you down. She has the phone in her hand.

'A call for you, detective,' she says. 'It's your captain from the squad room, he says it's urgent.'

Turn to page 70 to see what this is about.

By the time you get to the door, Walter has already bolted back down the corridor towards the main lobby. You give chase. He throws a pained look over his shoulder, his urgency picking up when he sees you're in pursuit.

An unfortunate waitress carrying a tray of plates and cutlery comes out of the kitchen at absolutely the wrong time. Walter hits her hard and the tray goes flying. She lets out a scream but he doesn't stop to help her. He continues down the hallway. You apologise as you step over her, some of her colleagues helping her back to her feet.

Walter shoulders the door of the hallway open. He's out, quick as a flash, as you try to catch up. The lobby opens up ahead of you when you push through the door. It takes you a moment to adjust to the sudden throng of people. But you quickly spot Walter making for the main doors.

Hurrying after him, you weave through the crowd. He's out the main doors and into the forecourt where the valet attendants are taking keys and cars. As you stumble out of the huge revolving doors of the Royale Premiere entranceway, you spot Walter. He snatches a set of keys from a hapless attendant and clambers into a sleek, brand-new Ferrari 250 California Spyder, its hood down to soak up the rays.

The engine, still running, roars as Walter guns the accelerator. Running as fast as you can, you throw yourself towards the sports car. You land hard on the back canopy. It's enough to distract Walter, just for a second. He looks around and sees you holding on. The wheel spins beyond his grip, foot planted on the gas. There's a screech as the tyres cry out for mercy before the whole car judders and slips off the smooth tarmac of the forecourt.

The crunch is both loud and painful as the beautiful car is crumpled – a tall pylon that holds up the concrete canopy of the forecourt making sure you're not going anywhere. The horn makes a pitiful wheeze as smoke begins to pour from the hood. You slip off the back, open the driver's side door and haul Walter out by the collar.

Valet attendants and other staff come rushing over to make sure everyone is okay. You throw the keys at the nearest one, telling them to apologise to the owner.

'Mr Walter?' asks one of the attendants.

He says nothing, rubbing his forehead where he collided with the steering wheel. You tell him he's lucky he wasn't going fast or far, otherwise the steering column would be through his face.

The commotion outside has caused a sudden rush of people out the main entrance way of the hotel. As the crowd moves to see what's happened, you slip back inside with Walter firmly in your grip. You make your way back to his office without a fuss and dump him into his chair.

'I think I've got a concussion,' he moans, rubbing the bright red mark on his forehead.

You slam your hands down on the desk in front of him. That's enough to shut him up. He looks at you with watery blue eyes. He's suddenly very small, timid almost, shoulders hunched up and spindly hands fumbling with each other. You pull out the switchblade you found in his desk and dump it down on the desk. Walter's face drops, wrinkles sagging on either side of his drooping, pencil moustache.

'What ... how did you—?'

- You let Walter explain himself on the following page

- You accuse him of murdering Blanche Aikerman on page 142

'Look, I know how this may come across, but believe me, I had nothing to do with Miss Aikerman's murder,' he says. 'This knife, it's just … it's been confiscated, from another member of staff.'

You say that all sounds rather convenient, given Blanche Aikerman was found with a cut throat.

'It's the truth, I swear to you,' says Walter. 'There was an incident, overnight, I wasn't here for it. Contrary to what my wife believes, I'm not here every hour of every day. I do take some time off, you know. Last night was one of those exceptions. With the Golden Star Awards in town, I knew I'd be here all weekend. And that was *before* this terrible business with Blanche. So I clocked off early last night and went home to have dinner with my wife and kids. You know, like a normal human being.'

He mops his brow of sweat. His shoulders release a little.

'Anyway, we ate and I was relaxing with a glass of Scotch when the phone rings,' he says. 'It must have been around ten, no later. It was the night manager. He said he had to break up a fight between a kitchen porter and one of our sous chefs. Apparently they'd been arguing over a recipe or something trivial. The porter pulled this and threatened the chef.'

He opens his hands, gesturing towards the switchblade on the desk.

'I said I had been drinking and didn't want to drive, not across this city at ten at night. I told the night manager to deal with it, fire the porter, offer the chef an extra fifty in his pay packet and leave the knife here in my desk for me to deal with in the morning. And that's what happened, I swear.'

He is pleading with you now. The story sounds perfectly plausible. You can't count how many fatal encounters you've dealt with in your career where petty disagreements turn into something more sinister. Bar fights, road rage, neighbourly disputes. In this city anything can turn into a homicide at the drop of a hat. A warring chef and their kitchen porter, it's plausible.

You're about to ask about the paperwork when Walter does something unexpected. Before you can react, he's grabbed the knife off the desk. As you're processing what's happening, he lunges at you from behind the desk. You try to get your hands up in time but it's too late. You feel the cool blade slide into your throat.

Coughing, choking, your legs going weak, you stumble backwards. Blood is pouring from the wound in your neck. Your hands are slick as you grasp at your throat. Lurching forward, Walter's desk fills your blurring view. Drops of your blood have fallen on the overdue bills and invoices, decorating them with bright scarlet. Your knees buckle and you drop to the floor while Walter stands over you.

'You asked too many questions, officer,' he says to you, chest heaving up and down. 'You should have looked in other places, questioned that awful old boot Mrs Aikerman or that Kraut, von Hiltz, who has me running around this place like a lackey mopping up his scandals. Any of them could have killed Blanche. And I'm not sorry if they did. But you shouldn't have interfered with my business, my debts. Now you're snuffed out. And my friends in the LA Mafia will have to save me again. Goodbye, officer. Thanks for nothing.'

You try to speak but only blood comes out, drowning any protests you may have in a crimson sea. Then the world begins to fade to darkness as death embraces you. The case ends here for you.

You gave Walter too much time and space to manoeuvre, not to mention trusting him more than you should. Perhaps taking a more direct approach on P142 will yield some results from Mr Walter.

'What? No! No, I didn't murder Blanche! I found her, well Carter found her, but I found her after that. I didn't kill her!'

There's a desperation to his voice. You ask him about the knife.

'This? It's not mine, I swear!' he shouts.

You don't seem convinced. Walter picks up on your scepticism. He takes a huge gulp of air.

'Look, I know how this may come across, but believe me, I had nothing to do with Blanche's murder,' he says. 'This knife, it's just … it's been confiscated, from another member of staff.'

You say that all sounds rather convenient, given Blanche Aikerman was found with a cut throat.

'It's the truth, I swear to you,' says Walter. 'There was an incident, overnight, I wasn't here for it. Contrary to what my wife believes, I'm not here every hour of every day. I do take some time off, you know. Last night was one of those exceptions. With the Golden Star Awards in town, I knew I'd be here all weekend. And that was *before* this terrible business with Blanche. So I clocked off early last night and went home to have dinner with my wife and kids. You know, like a normal human being.'

He mops his brow of sweat. His shoulders release a little.

'Anyway, we ate and I was relaxing with a glass of Scotch when the phone rings,' he says. 'It must have been around ten, no later. It was the night manager. He said he had to break up a fight between a kitchen porter and one of our sous chefs. Apparently they'd been arguing over a recipe or something trivial. The porter pulled this and threatened the chef.'

He opens his hands, gesturing towards the switchblade on the desk.

'I said I had been drinking and didn't want to drive, not across this city at ten at night. I told the night manager to deal with it, fire the porter, offer the chef an extra fifty in his pay packet and leave the knife here in my desk for me to deal with in the morning. And that's what happened, I swear.'

He is pleading with you now. The story sounds perfectly plausible. You can't count how many fatal encounters you've dealt with in your career where petty disagreements turn into something more sinister. Bar fights, road rage, neighbourly disputes. In this city anything can turn into a homicide at the drop of a hat. A warring chef and their kitchen porter, it's plausible.

You gesture down at the paperwork and receipts you found in the drawer. Walter's face flushes with embarrassment.

'I'd rather not discuss these, if that's all right,' he says.

You remind him that you are a LAPD homicide detective on a murder case. And that as it stands, you've found a potential murder weapon in his drawer and he has a wafer-thin alibi. That seems to shock him into speaking.

'I'm … in debt,' he says. 'And when I say debt, I mean I owe a fortune. These bills, notices, they're all for me. And quite frankly, I'm in way over my head with some quite nasty people.'

Walter looks close to tears. He clears his throat and begins leafing through the receipts and folder.

'It all started when I was around sixteen,' he says. 'I won my first five bucks when I picked the right horse at our local downs. It was a nasty little place, full of unsavoury characters, I'm sure you know the type, detective. My father, he used to take my brother and I. He was a deadbeat, a bum. I shouldn't have been so surprised. What kind of dad takes his kids to the track? He spent and lost every last penny he had at this place, just outside Portland in Oregon. I guess when you grow up around that kind of environment, you develop a taste for it. I'm only surprised it took me so long to finally pluck up the courage to place my first bet. I was underage of course, but the cashier didn't care. Why would she. It was a dollar, like any other. And the more they take, the easier their lives are with the house upstairs. Anyway, the horse came in. I was so elated. I'd never felt a rush like it. To have five bucks in my pocket, I'd never seen so much money. My father was happy, for about ten minutes. Then he wanted the cash to bet some more. I refused and he beat me, of course, took the money back and lost it on the very next race. I should have learned then, as a teenager, that this was a slippery slope. *What's the old saying? The apple never falls far from the tree. Like father, like son, all of those cliches.* I never stood a chance, when I look back on it now. His gambling was always there in every part of my life, our lives as a family. Of course I didn't learn, no gambler ever does. And that's the problem, detective. Gambling, it's not about the winning, far from it. It's the *losing* that keeps us coming back for more and more and more, until we have nothing left. If you gave me a roulette wheel that was rigged and told me every time where the ball would land, I wouldn't be interested.

Where's the risk in that? I'm an addict, like my old man, I just knew how to hide it better than he ever did.'

Walter wipes away a tear from his eye.

'The problem with addiction, detective, is that you think you've got it beat when deep down you know it'll never go away. And the older you get, the more respected you are, like I am here at the Royale Premiere, the bigger the risk and the greater the stakes. The more money that appears in your pocket book, the more likely you are to spin it on a game of chance or the cards. That's what's happened to me. To the outside world I'm a success. But behind closed doors, I'm a wreck. I don't know why my family still puts up with me. Pity, I suppose, or they're just as crazy as I am. If they only knew *half* of what I've done to keep the wolves from the door, they'd be ashamed and string me up. And I'd deserve it, too. Of course I would. It's a problem, I know, but I just can't stop,' he says, waving the overdue bills at you.

He scatters the files and papers across the desk. His shoulders sink now and he's hunched over, a defeated man. His pristine shirt, tie and jacket look far too big on him. There's a clown quality to his appearance now, where before he strode around the hotel like a Roman Emperor.

You ask who he owes money too and how the hotel is involved.

'I've been syphoning off funds from different departments,' he says. 'Not to gamble with, just to pay off my debts. The owners don't know, they don't care really. This place is a goldmine, this weekend will take six figures alone, just from hosting the Golden Star Awards. As for who I owe money too, well, that's sort of self-explanatory, isn't it?'

You ask for specifics. Walter gets up from behind his desk. You watch him, aware that there's a very dangerous knife sitting out, just within grabbing distance. He looks out of the door and then closes it, conspiratorially.

'Silvio Boffi,' he says. 'Also known as The Hammer. I don't need to tell a police officer that he's one of the LA Mafia's top men. Apart from being a bloodthirsty creep, he's also a patron of the Royale Premiere board. Legitimate businessman is how he describes himself. But believe me, there's absolutely nothing legitimate about Boffi, or that Gun Moll of his. Do you know she has the audacity to be staying here this weekend, like she's one of the Hollywood crowd. She's even taken the honeymoon suite. Although I doubt her husband is with her. He wouldn't be seen dead with this crowd.'

Walter nods his head towards the door. There's a lot to take in here. Especially Walter's involvement with gangsters. You find that you have a number of options to pursue.

- You ask where Silvio 'The Hammer' Boffi's moll is staying in the

  hotel – looking to speak with her on page 149

- You ask Walter why he returned to his underused office when he

  learned of Blanche's murder on the next page

The manager of the Royale Premiere clears his throat. He opens the door of the office a crack and makes sure there is nobody on the other side listening. When he's satisfied, he gently clicks the door closed. You find this all a little strange. Walter seems to pick up on your curiosity.

'I'm sorry,' he says. 'I just wanted to make sure there was nobody about. What I'm about to show you isn't exactly my proudest moment as the manager of this place. But it has to be done, unfortunately.'

Again, you're not quite sure what Walter is up to. Your thoughts quickly turn back to the knife on the table. It's a lethal weapon just there to be used. You try and manoeuvre yourself between the hotel manager and the blade. Just in case.

Walter moves across the cramped little office to the far wall. He runs his finger under the edge of the frame of the giant painting of the Royale Premiere. You hear a click and he swings the portrait outward, revealing a safe built into the wall. Walter turns the dial, clicking the combination code into place. The door opens and he stands to one side, his head bowed.

You step forward, looking at the safe. There, in the middle of more paperwork, stands a glistening Golden Star Award statue. It's like a beacon, a shiny ray of light among the dismal setting of Walter's office. The light above your head catches on the curves and art deco angles of the famous gong – a depiction of Icarus in solid gold, his wings spread wide. You reach in and take the statue out of the safe. A small plaque is inscribed beneath the Greek hero's feet. It reads 'Best Actress 1958 – Blanche Aikerman'.

You show the statue to Walter. He looks ashamed.

'I'm sorry,' he says. 'But I'm desperate. When I found out that Blanche had been murdered, I thought of nothing else but the award she was going to get tomorrow night. That's a piece of Hollywood history you're holding in your hands, detective. Those statues fetch tens of thousands of dollars on the black market. Now that Blanche has been savagely murdered, anything and everything she's been associated with, even remotely, will skyrocket in value. As for that award, it's the Golden Star she never won, the stuff of fable, of myth.'

He takes the gong from you. Cradling it, like a newborn, he stares wistfully down at it in his hands.

'This could have been my ticket to freedom,' he says. 'I didn't think twice, not at all. After I saw Blanche just lying there, I thought about these statues. They're kept in a safe, under lock and key and an armed guard at the back of the conference centre where the awards will take place tomorrow night. Only a handful of people have access, myself, the awards committee, that sort of thing. Nobody would think twice about the manager of the Royale Premiere wanting to inspect the awards the day before the ceremony, to make sure everything is in check. So that's what I did. And when I was alone, I took Blanche's award. As soon as I could, I would have put it through a fence. God knows how much I would have got for it in the end. But it would have been more than enough to clear my debt with The Hammer.'

You reach out to take the statue back. Walter is a little hesitant at first. Then he relinquishes the gong. You carefully tuck the award into the pocket of your trench coat. It weighs you down to one side and you adjust yourself.

'What are you going to do now?' asks Walter.

You explain to him that he's going to have to be arrested for theft, at the very least. Not to mention the reckless driving earlier and the evading arrest. He bows his head again and nods.

'I thought as much,' he says.

You collect the switchblade and lead Walter out of his office. You keep a loose grip on his arm as you make your way back out to the main lobby of the hotel. Seeing the manager of the Royale Premiere being escorted by the police does, inevitably, draw attention. There are hushed sighs as the crowd spot what's going on.

'Please,' says Walter, quietly to you. 'Don't make me stand here with everyone gawping.'

You acknowledge his request and lead him to the front doors. Outside, a couple of police cruisers are on the scene. You snag one of the uniformed cops and flash your badge. You tell him to take Mr Walter into custody and he immediately slaps handcuffs on the hotel manager. As he's about to lead him away, you also, subtly pass him Blanche Aikerman's Goldie. His eyes almost drop out of his head.

'Holy cow,' he says, breathless.

You also pass over the switchblade and tell the officer that it's all evidence, that Mr Walter will cooperate when he's taken back to the station. The hotel manager nods in agreement.

'Of course,' says the uniformed cop. 'Right away.'

He gently guides Walter away to a waiting police cruiser. You watch as the door is closed firmly on Walter. He gives you a sad look, just the faintest of smiles creeping across his thin lips. There's a resignation to him now, if not total relief. The police cruiser pulls away.

You're about to turn back into the hotel when you notice there are two, tall, mean-looking men in smart suits standing either side of you. You're certain they weren't there before. One of them, chewing on a toothpick, leans in close to you. His breath is hot and smells of fried onions.

'Shame to see Mr Walter go like that,' he says. 'Mr Boffi's wife would like to have a word with you, if that's not too much trouble, officer.'

The heavy is smiling, or as close to a smile as someone with a slab of meat for a face can conjure up. His colleague isn't much better, a large scar running from the bridge of his nose down to the corner of his cheek.

- You agree to go with Boffi's heavies on the next page

- You ignore Boffi's heavies and start to walk away on

  page 151

'What are you going to do now?' asks Walter.

You explain to him that he's going to have to be arrested for theft, at the very least. Not to mention the reckless driving earlier and the evading arrest. He bows his head again and nods.

'I thought as much,' he says.

You collect the switchblade and lead Walter out of his office. You keep a loose grip on his arm as you make your way back out to the main lobby of the hotel. Seeing the manager of the Royale Premiere being escorted by the police does, inevitably, draw attention. There are hushed sighs as the crowd spot what's going on.

'Please,' says Walter, quietly to you. 'Don't make me stand here with everyone gawping.'

You acknowledge his request and lead him to the front doors. Outside, a couple of police cruisers are on the scene, dealing with the crash from earlier. You snag one of the uniformed cops and flash your badge. You tell him to take Mr Walter into custody and he immediately slaps handcuffs on the hotel manager. You also pass over the switchblade and tell the officer that Mr Walter will cooperate when he's taken back to the station house. The hotel manager nods in agreement.

'Of course,' says the uniformed cop. 'Right away.'

He gently guides Walter away to a waiting police cruiser. You watch as the door is closed firmly on Walter. He gives you a sad look, just the faintest of smiles creeping across his thin lips. There's a resignation to him now, if not total relief. The police cruiser pulls away.

You're about to turn back into the hotel when you notice there are two, tall, mean-looking men in smart suits standing either side of you. You're certain they weren't there before. One of them, chewing a toothpick, leans in close to you. His breath is hot and smells of fried onions.

'Shame to see Mr Walter go like that,' he says. 'Mr Boffi's wife would like to have a word with you, if that's not too much trouble, officer.'

The heavy is smiling, or as close to a smile as someone with a slab of meat for a face can conjure up. His colleague isn't much better, a large scar running from the bridge of his nose down to the corner of his cheek.

It wouldn't be wise to get on the wrong side of these neanderthals. You agree to meet with their boss on page 153.

You've barely taken a step when you feel a hand on your shoulder. You look down at it. Big, meaty fingers are digging into you. Beneath the fur are tattoos spelling out 'HATE' across the knuckles. You look up at Toothpick who is still smiling.

'I really think it would be in your best interest to come with us, officer,' he says. 'Mrs Boffi doesn't like to be kept waiting.'

You shrug off his hand and march back into the hotel. Before you can cross the lobby, you find you've been lifted an inch off the ground. The heavies are either side of you again but this time, their hands lift you up by your armpits. They move quickly, efficiently, making sure nobody sees what's going on. You're hustled through a door marked 'staff' and down a hallway. At the other end is an exit that leads to a back loading yard.

A group of cooks are sitting smoking in the far corner of the courtyard. They're playing cards on an upturned wooden crate. Toothpick whistles and snaps his fingers. The cooks don't hesitate. They quickly get up and hurry back into the hotel, leaving the cards and dollar bills on their makeshift table.

When the place is quiet, Toothpick and Scar drop you back onto your feet. You adjust your coat sleeves. As you're about to ask what's going on, Scar aims a well-placed fist into your stomach. It knocks the wind out of you immediately and you double over.

'Mrs Boffi doesn't like what you've been doing here today,' says Toothpick. 'She thinks you might be causing some undue harassment to one of her marks.'

He kicks you in the ribs, sending you rolling across the yard.

'And when Mrs Boffi is upset, we get upset, right?'

Scar grunts something inaudible. He cracks his knuckles as they both walk towards you. You can't breathe, you feel like your throat has been stuffed with cotton buds. Tears are blurring your vision. Your first thought is to reach for your gun. But Toothpick is faster and grabs it first.

'We don't want any trouble, officer, honest,' he says, clicking the hammer of your pistol. 'Only, if Mr Walter goes down to your station, there's a real good chance that he starts saying things that we really don't want him to be saying. And we can't have that, can we?'

He kneels down beside you, jamming the barrel of the gun into your temple.

'You wouldn't want anything nasty to happen to Mrs Boffi would you, officer? She's an upstanding member of the Los Angeles community. Being associated with common criminals like Walter wouldn't do her reputation any good, would it?'

You can't answer, still fighting to catch your breath.

'That's why this has to end here,' he says, his crooked smile dropping, flat forehead lowered down over his eyes. 'No more questions. No more implications. Just another dead cop on the mean streets of LA. A real shame.'

That draws a laugh from Scar. Your breath is just returning when you hear the almighty roar of your gun going off. Then there's nothing.

The case ends here for you. But you can always start again by turning to Chapter 1.

Toothpick and Scar gently but firmly guide you back into the hotel. You try to make eye contact with some of the LAPD loitering about around the crash, but they don't seem to see you. The heavies are discreet. They move you across the lobby. Nobody seems to notice you as you pass through the crowds. Perhaps it's the boxers' noses and broad chests that keep anyone from making eye contact with your hosts.

They lead you up a flight of broad steps at the very back of the lobby. A long row of heavy doors are in front of you with the sign 'Main Theatre' in large, gold letters above them. Pushing through, they escort you into the amphitheatre of the Royale Premiere.

Row after row of red velvet seats all lead down towards the main stage. The last preparations are being made to the staging for tomorrow night's Golden Star Awards. A giant replica of the gong dominates the left of the stage. A huge, golden Icarus, depicted with his wings spread wide. It's rather imposing.

There is, however, another more distracting presence on the stage. A woman stands with her back to the audience section. She's in the middle of the stage, a lone figure among all the glitz and glamour. Her emerald dress is sparkling, even in the shadows, a large open curve that reveals her smooth back all the way down to the nape. A white fur throw is draped about her shoulders and you can just about see a mop of chestnut curls resting on top.

As the heavies hustle you down the centre aisle of the auditorium, a great beam of light suddenly engulfs her. She slowly turns around, bathed in the luminescence. Even from down here you can see her beauty. A round and neat face framed by her short curls, piercing blue eyes and lips as red as blood. She puffs on a cigarette, the smoke curling about her like a python before disappearing into the light. You suspect that Mrs Boffi knew you were here, long before you set eyes on her. She has the air of confidence about her that only movie stars earn when they're world famous. Only she's not a movie star. Far from it. She's a gangster's moll. And she knows it.

'Lovely to see you, detective,' she says, her voice smooth, confident. 'Camilla Boffi. I'd shake your hand but I'm enjoying the limelight too much. Don't you think it suits me?'

She does a spin. The sequins on her dress sparkle, sending spectrums of colour all around the stage. You don't get a chance to answer. Instead the heavies bundle you to the side of the stage and force you up the steps. To think that some of Hollywood's great and good will be making the same journey in a few hours time crosses your mind. These, however, are *very* different circumstances.

'I thought I'd give this place a little dry run before it all gets underway,' says Boffi. 'It's a shame to leave all this hard work and nobody use it.'

'I'm sorry if my boys were a little rough with you, detective,' she says. 'They don't play well with others. Am I right?'

'Blunt instruments, but sometimes you have to be to the point in his business,' says Boffi. 'I'm not going to insult our intelligence by asking if you know who my husband is, detective.'

'Good,' says Boffi, drawing on her cigarette. 'Then you'll know that it's probably not a good idea to go poking your nose in his affairs. You're just lucky I'm here and not him – workers' dispute in New Jersey keeping him away from all the action.'

You look about the stage. Everything is almost complete and ready for the ceremony. You can't help but wonder what someone like Boffi would have to do with this world. It feels like a million miles away from intimidation and racketeering. Then again, Blanche Aikerman is lying with her throat cut in her bedroom. Maybe showbusiness isn't *that* different from organised crime.

'A little bird tells me you've been harassing one of my favourite clients,' says Boffi. 'Mr Walter, the manager of this fine establishment. You know that's naughty, officer, and likely to get you in all sorts of trouble.'

'I'm no cop, far from it. But I reckon you shaking down Walter is something to do with Blanche Aikerman's murder. Am I right?'

How do you react here?

- You keep your cool with Boffi on the next page

- You tell Boffi that she's right on page 173

You keep your cool. You tell Boffi that you're a homicide detective and that you have a duty to uphold the law, no matter what that takes.

'Very admirable of you, detective,' she says, taking long, elegant strides across the stage, circling you like a vulture and carrion. 'That still doesn't explain why poor, dear Blanche has been killed.'

Thinking quickly, you try to turn the tide of the conversation. You ask Boffi why she would think Blanche has been murdered. And even if that is the case, how would she know something like that?

'Ah,' Boffi smiles, showing her perfect teeth. 'Very good, detective. Very good indeed. Makes me think you like a little game of poker on the side, when the captain isn't looking. You'd clean up with that bluffing of yours. Walk with me.'

She curls her finger as she stalks off towards the side of the stage. You follow, Toothpick and Scar remaining at a safe but present distance behind. Some stage hands and staff see Boffi coming and quickly clear out of the way. Nobody, it seems, wants to be within ten feet of her. From what you know of her husband's reputation, you can understand why. Being a cop, however, doesn't give you that luxury.

'Do you like what we're doing with the place?' she asks, lifting her hands to show off the staging and set for the awards. 'I still have to pinch myself that I've got a say in all of this. Imagine that, a street rat from Brooklyn deciding who gets the most prestigious and coveted awards in Hollywood. You couldn't write it, detective, honestly you couldn't. Anyone who took my story on would make a million bucks overnight. The box office would be smashed. Only they don't like my kind out here in California. I'm a bit too real for them, remind these sun-tanned phonies that back east there are real problems, real issues, real-life heroes and villains. Everything has to be false here in Hollywood. Why do you think I'm trussed up like a peacock in heat?'

Boffi weaves her way through the backstage area. Her glistening emerald dress is a stark contrast to the down and dirty surroundings. Boxes, crates, ropes, levers, rigging, everything seems to bend around her as she moves. If flowers sprung from the floor where she walked, you wouldn't be surprised. Camilla Boffi is that rare thing: dangerous, deadly, utterly charming.

'You're keeping your cards close to your chest, detective, and I respect that,' she says. 'But I don't have to remind you who my husband is. The Hammer, he loves that name, loves the infamy. It's me who has to deal with his business and numbers. Poor Silvio can barely write his own name, let alone run an empire. That's why I'm telling you that if somebody has been whacked in this city, there's a good chance I'm going to know about it. And, more importantly, know who did it.'

She comes to a stop at a dressing table. The bright lights that surround the mirror bathe her. She picks up a lipstick from the tabletop and begins to adjust her make-up. She looks at you in the mirror while she puckers up.

'Do you know who killed Blanche Aikerman?' she asks flatly.

You take a deep breath. This is all very unconventional, not to mention dangerous. Camilla Boffi is a known Mafia figure. You don't make deals with criminals. All the while, you're also very aware of how high-profile this murder case is. If there's any chance that Boffi can help, surely you'd be mad not to take it. *Right?*

You decide to take the diplomatic approach. You say that, if the rumours of Blanche Aikerman's demise are true, then any and all information relating to the case would be appreciated by the LAPD. And that withholding information could lead to potential charges.

The last statement makes Boffi laugh. She puts down her lipstick, turns on her expensive heels and winks.

'I like it when you cops talk dirty,' she says.

She looks over your shoulder. Flicking her head the tiniest amount, she signals to the heavies to go. You watch them leave, moving back towards the main stage. You are alone with Camilla Boffi.

'You know, I think we'd both be in trouble if my husband found out I was even *speaking* to you,' she says, slowly walking towards you, all hips and smoky eyes. 'The Hammer has this thing against cops. It's not a phobia, he's not scared of the boys in blue. It's just this, I don't know, uncontrollable hatred that turns him mad as hell whenever he even hears you spoken about.'

You feel this is turning into a trap.

'Just as well he's back in New Jersey sorting out a workers' dispute, huh?'

She walks around you. She dances her fingers on your shoulder, never taking her eyes from you. When she comes full circle, she stops.

'So, that all being said,' she says. 'If I was going to help you, detective. What's in it for me, given I'm risking my neck?'

You remind Boffi that you're a cop and that any deals have to be run past your captain.

'Pish posh,' she says, pouting. 'Have you always been such a square?'

She stomps back over to the dressing table and snatches up a lighter and packet of cigarettes. Stealing one, she sparks it and leans on the table, smiling.

'I thought you homicide detectives were a lot more fun,' she says.

You don't react. She's still smiling. Tapping ash onto the floor, she lets the smoke dance around her head. It's just as hypnotised as you are.

'I'll level with you, detective,' she says. 'I don't know who killed Blanche Aikerman. Yeah, yeah, I know you can't say that's true for official reasons. I get it. But I know. You can't sneeze or step on a turd in this town without me knowing. Facts of life. What I *do* know is that your Mr Walter had nothing to do with it. I'm not an alibi or anything but I know the man. He's a gambler, a loser, one of life's hard-luck cases who wallows in his own misery. He's desperate, sure. He owes my husband a *lot* of money. That said, he's not capable of killing anyone, let alone Blanche Aikerman. He's not *that* desperate. You're barking up the wrong tree if you think that's the case, detective. And I think you're smarter than that.'

She sucks hard on the cigarette, the fire burning bright at the end. The smoke blows from her nostrils and she licks her teeth, picking out a stray strand of tobacco.

'What I *will* say is that Blanche Aikerman was no angel, she didn't have the opportunity to be,' says Boffi. 'She's a young woman trying to make her way in this industry. That's not easy, believe me, detective. The amount of crap you have to deal with on a daily basis is enough to make you want to give the whole thing up at the first chance. I didn't know the girl, not really, not like some of the others here. Her mother was always very protective of her, always at her side. And let's be honest, having a gangster's wife hanging round isn't good for selling movie tickets. But I know what she was going through, as so many of these young up-and-comers are, men and women. This industry, it'll chew you up and spit you out and not call back in the morning. If you ask me, and I know you're not, but if you ask me, you might want to take a look at that director pal of hers. What's his name, the German, von Hiltz?'

You ask why Boffi has a problem with Peter von Hiltz. She taps the side of her nose.

'Rumours, detective, that's all,' she says. 'This town is built on hearsay and conjecture. It's all about reputation. Why do you think my two boys are standing just behind that curtain there when I told them to scram?'

She nods to the curtain just to your right. Toothpick and Scar appear, right on cue.

'Reputation. They know that if they went as far as six inches from my side, leaving me alone with a cop, I'd have their balls for Christmas tree decorations. Ain't that right boys?'

The heavies laugh. It sounds like the start of an earthquake. They sidle up to you, Toothpick on your left, Scar to the right.

'Like I said, reputation.' Boffi laughs, crushing out her cigarette. 'And that's what this von Hiltz character has. A reputation. It's not the best, nobody is squeaky clean, except maybe you, detective. Peter von Hiltz is known to be tricky to work with. Nobody worked more with him than Blanche Aikerman. Doesn't take one of these NASA boffins to work out there might be some animosity there.'

You ask Boffi if she thinks von Hiltz killed Blanche.

'I don't know,' she says. 'But I've seen people kill for a lot less. I've seen men murder their wives because their dinner was cold. I've seen moms toss their babies in the trash because they can't cope with the crying, the screaming. I've seen it all, detective, and Hollywood wants nothing to do with any of it. Ask our German friend what he *really* thinks of Blanche Aikerman and you might start getting some answers. You'll get nothing from Walter.'

Boffi straightens. She wipes away stray ash from the front of her glittering frock. A sense of business comes across her, gone is the alluring, provocative femme fatale.

'Now, we have just the small matter of payment to discuss,' she says.

Toothpick and Scar get a little closer to you.

'Don't look so surprised, detective,' she laughs. 'I'm not telling you all this for the good of my health. The way I see it, you have a straight choice. In exchange for my services, you can either let Walter go. Or you can take your chances with my boys here. Either way, don't leave me hanging, I've still got a ton of work to do with these awards, even if the star of the show has been snuffed out.'

She puts her hands on her hips and cocks her head to the side. It's clear you have a choice to make.

- You agree that you'll have a word with your captain about Walter

  on the next page ★

- You refuse, saying the LAPD doesn't make deals with criminals

  like Boffi on page 166

'See,' she says, wagging a finger. 'I knew you were one of the smart ones. I can always tell these things. It comes with growing up around cops. Some of you have that honest streak that runs through you. You're straight arrows, can't be bought, won't stray from the truth and justice and all that. Then there's the fat cats who grow rich and lazy on kickbacks. They're my favourite. You can always buy them off with a fifty here and there, get them to look the other way. Doesn't matter which way, just not at me. They're sweeties.'

You feel a little cheap as Boffi talks about the LAPD that way. Unfortunately, you know she's right. There have been, and remain, too many officers, detectives, even captains, who have had their palms greased by mobsters like Boffi and her crew. It's a way of life, a necessary evil. You've seen the caseloads that Internal Affairs deal with. You wouldn't wish that job on your worst enemy.

This all feels like you're flying way too close to the sun. You eye the giant Icarus statue at the side of the stage and feel suddenly sympathetic. Agreeing to speak with Captain Barclay about Walter's arrests, it's all dirty and murky. But you're investigating the murder of the most famous woman in the world. And time is pressing. You can't make an omelette without breaking a few eggs, as your old mother used to say.

'Where do you think I got my boys from?' Boffi laughs.

You throw a quick glance at Toothpick and Scar. Hard to believe that they were once cops like you. Then again, if they're in this line of work now, they were *never* a cop like you.

You tell Boffi that you'll put a call into the station about Walter. He won't be back there yet so no paperwork will have been filed. She takes a small bow.

'You're a star,' she says.

There's a change in her tone now. It feels less amicable, more businesslike. Almost like she's tired of entertaining you or even having you in her company.

'Well, detective, I think you've got an awful lot to do,' she says. 'Murderers don't catch themselves, do they?'

She's right. Toothpick and Scar step forward. It's clear now that your audience with Camilla Boffi has come to an end.

You're unsure if you should thank her or not. It doesn't feel right somehow, so you don't. She doesn't seem at all bothered.

The heavies escort you back to the main stage and down into the central aisle between the red-velvet chairs. They stop at the doorway that leads out to the main lobby of the Royale Premiere. You're about to step through when Boffi calls to you from the stage.

'Remember, detective, I know *everything* that goes on in this town,' she winks at you. 'Don't forget about our little arrangement now, will you? I'd hate to have to send the boys around to that station house of yours and remind you of our deal. And remember, honey, I make Capone look like a cuddly teddy bear.'

There's something chilling to her words, despite the broad, perfect smile on her face. She blows you a kiss and you head out of the door. It slams closed behind you, Toothpick and Scar safely on the other side. You don't mind admitting quietly to yourself that you're glad to see them gone. There was something unsettling about those pair, even to a hardened cop like you.

You clear your head. You suspect that Captain Barclay, your superior officer, isn't going to like what you've got to say regarding Walter or Camilla Boffi. Needs must, unfortunately. And it's within your right and duty to use any means possible to catch a murderer on the loose.

As you're about to head down the stairs that lead to the theatre, somebody catches your eye. Among all the hubbub of the main lobby and entrance of the Royale Premiere, a lone figure stands out like a sore thumb. Victor Ramsay – studio executive at Thundersaga Pictures, where Blanche Aikerman was a star.

He's not somebody you know directly. But he's almost as famous as the actors, producers and directors he employs. The pictures in the newspapers and film reels don't do the mogul justice. He is, in real life, much larger than anything you could have imagined.

Well over six feet tall and almost the same in width, he walks with a commanding confidence, every step feeling like it shudders the ground. His suit is huge, acres of fabric cut, sliced and stitched together in the latest fashion. It's the only part of him that appears human, everything else is enlarged and, strangely, grotesque. From his bulging eyes and slab of meat for a head to his pursed lips, slightly blue, and comically small ears, Victor Ramsay barrels across the lobby of the Royale Premiere like the *Titanic* on its maiden voyage.

Remembering what Boffi told you, that Blanche was a young woman trying to make her way in this notoriously difficult industry, you wonder how much Ramsay knows.

Where does your investigation take you now?

- Forget about Boffi and run after Ramsay on the following

  page

- Keep your deal with Boffi and head to the reception desk in the

  hotel on page 165

'Can I help you?' he asks.

Ramsay is much taller when you get up close to him. It feels like you're staring up at a mountain. You flash your badge. His tone doesn't change. There's an intimidation about him but it's only from his sheer size. His voice is controlled, his manner polite.

'Is something wrong, officer?' he asks.

You decide that this is far too public a place to be conducting this kind of conversation. Although the Moon would still be too small a space to speak with someone like Victor Ramsay. You politely usher him away from the peering queue at reception to a quieter alcove further in the lobby.

Carry on your conversation with Ramsay on page 64.

Weaving through the gathered crowd. It's like swimming against the current as the whole lobby area is jam-packed with people. The staff of the Royale Premiere are having just as difficult a time as you trying to navigate across their place of work. You have every sympathy for them. It's only going to get worse as the weekend draws on and more and more people descend on the venue. That is unless the murder of Blanche Aikerman cancels everything. The thought makes you panic. Camilla Boffi doesn't strike you as the kind of person who takes bad news well.

You finally reach the reception desk. A friendly staff member greets you with a large smile. You're about to ask her for help when she holds up a telephone.

'It's a call for you, officer,' she says. 'It's your squad room, an urgent call.'

Take the call from the squad room on page 70.

Boffi sucks her tongue. She shakes her head, folding her arms across her sparkly chest.

'Dear oh dear oh dear,' she says. 'And there was me thinking that you were a smart cookie. Such a shame, detective. I kind of liked you.'

She snaps her fingers. Toothpick and Scar are on you, grabbing you by the shoulders. You anticipate the heavies and are able to reach into your holster and pull out your pistol.

'Gun!' Boffi screams.

The heavies wrestle your arm. You get a shot off, the bullet flying into the rafters and pinging off something metal. Boffi ducks for cover, sheltering behind the dressing table and mirror.

'Get his shooter you idiots!' she shouts.

Toothpick curses, Scar snarls. You try to remember your basic training from the police academy. There was nothing in there about wrestling with two shaved apes. It's time to improvise.

You let off another shot. The bullet smashes into the mirror, showering Boffi in broken glass. More importantly, your revolver explodes right next to Toothpick's ear. His grip loosens for a second as he paws at the gnarled skin on the side of his meat-slab head. It's enough for you to break free. Rounding your pistol, you smash the handle into the bridge of Scar's nose. He makes a grunt as blood spurts from a gaping wound in the middle of his face. He staggers back, freeing you completely.

'Don't let him get away!' Boffi shouts.

You ignore her, bolting as quickly as you can back towards the main stage area. Toothpick and Scar rally and are in hot pursuit. Their cumbersome frames, wrapped up tightly in immaculate suits big enough to be a galleon's sails, aren't as fast as you. They rumble through the backstage area like a pair of giant boulders.

You dash onto the stage. Ahead of you the huge version of the Golden Star Icarus rears skyward. You hurry over to it and round its back. Toothpick and Scar are right behind. You duck and weave, trying to throw them off, using the statue as cover. The heavies aren't the brightest tools in the box, they don't realise they can flank you from either side. You don't hang around and shoulder the base of the statue.

The Icarus is surprisingly light – another Hollywood phoney. It wobbles a little before spilling forward, the base of the prop not fastened to the stage floor. Scar lets out a yelp before the whole thing lands on top of him. Prop it may be, but it's heavy and cumbersome enough to take him out.

'You bastard!' Toothpick yells. 'He was my cousin!'

Incensed, Toothpick lunges forward, trying to grab you. You duck out of the way and roll off the stage. Scrambling to your feet, you hurry up the central aisle. You need back-up, in a big way, there's bound to be some outside.

As you're hurrying away from the stage, a bullet whistles past your head. Then another. And a third. The bullets bury themselves in the velvet seats, puffs of stuffing appearing like rabbits' tails. You look over your shoulders. A dishevelled Camilla Boffi is on the stage, aiming a Derringer at your head. She screams something distinctly awful that would even make her hardened mobster husband blush as you barge through one of the main doors of the amphitheatre.

Leaping down the stairs two at a time, Toothpick isn't far behind. The anger must be fuelling his legs as he bears down on you. You hustle through the crowd, nobody at all interested in the fact you're being chased by this three-hundred-pound monster. Shoving your way out the main doors, you're relieved when you spot some LAPD uniforms still dealing with the crash and traffic from earlier.

You flash your badge just as Toothpick comes hurtling towards you. The officers stop him, drawing their guns. He skids to a halt before swearing at you. You catch your breath, instructing the officers to put him under arrest. As they slap cuffs on Toothpick, Camilla Boffi comes running out of the main entrance.

Her eyes go wide and wild when they see that her minder has been cuffed.

'You're making a *big* mistake, detective!' she screams, not caring about the scene she's creating. 'Wait until my husband hears about this!'

You give the signal and the uniforms grab the gun moll. A quick frisk and her Derringer drops to the ground. If she wasn't wearing so much make-up, you'd be sure she would be blushing.

'Just you wait,' she says as she's bundled towards a cruiser. 'Just you wait until my husband hears about this. You're dead. You're *all* dead!'

The door is slammed shut but you can still hear her muffled threats. You tip the brim of your hat skyward and puff out your cheeks. This hasn't turned into the kind of day you thought it would.

Boffi is being transported to the station – what's next for you?

- This criminal is too important not to escort back to the station

  and you jump into the car on the next page

- You leave Boffi to be booked by the other detectives at the station and head back into the hotel to see if you can discover

  anything else on page 171

You snag one of the passing officers and tell them to lock down the penthouse level. Whispering quietly, you tell them that there's been a murder and that nothing can contaminate the scene before the lab techs and photographers get here. You say that you're going to fetch them and will be back after you've booked Camilla Boffi.

The young officer's face is ashen white. They nod, agree and hurry off into the hotel with their instructions. You climb into the passenger seat as another uniform gets behind the wheel. You instruct them to take you back to the station house.

'You must have a screw loose to think this is going to fly, detective!' Boffi shouts from the back seat. 'Don't you know who I am? I *own* the whole West Coast!'

You set off away from the hotel. The early evening traffic on Sunset Boulevard is starting to build up. The driver turns on his siren and you start making good time. The blocks of Los Angeles whizz past.

'I was trying to do you a favour, too,' Boffi sneers. 'And what thanks do I get for my efforts. Cuffs and a ticket. No wonder people don't trust cops. You're all rotten at heart. Bought off with a fifty and a box of doughnuts.'

You're about to turn and chastise Boffi when you notice the driver has missed a turn. You ask what's going on but get a punch in the face instead. Reeling, you recoil back in the passenger seat. Tears blur your vision as you try to get your bearings. You hear Boffi laughing in the back seat.

'Like I said,' she cackles. 'Rotten to the core.'

The car skids around a corner, much too fast. You rattle around in your seat, bumping your head off the door. Your eyelids grow heavy but you fight the urge to pass out. The corrupt driver, one of Boffi's pawns, smashes a fist into your stomach and your breath vanishes. Coughing and choking, the car comes to a halt. The driver gets out, frees Boffi then opens your door. You spill out onto the dusty gravel.

A jet engine roars overhead and you look about. Los Angeles International Airport is a few hundred yards away. A huge plane descends from the heavens, landing with a skid on the runway. You've never been so close to an aircraft as you slowly get to your feet. Boffi and the corrupt officer are waiting for you, guns drawn.

You lean against the cruiser, head reeling, chest on fire. You taste blood from your broken nose.

'All you had to do was say "yes", detective,' says Boffi, her emerald sparkling dress billowing in the wind of the open field close to the runway. 'I was throwing you a bone. I thought you were smart, I thought you had something behind your eyes. Not just another do-gooder try-hard that doesn't think the cards are stacked against them. Like I said, I *own* the West Coast, and the LAPD, too. They're always happy to oblige if I ever need a helping hand. You should have taken the offer when it was given to you. Shame. I liked you.'

You try to speak but your throat has closed up, breath short. It's no use, anyway. Camilla Boffi has already made up her mind. She fires her pistol and the bullet hits you in the chest. The corrupt officer shoots, too, another three puncture wounds in your shoulder, abdomen and leg. You drop down in a heap among the dust and bleached shrub.

You lie staring up at the bronze sky of the LA evening. Then the darkness takes you forever.

The case ends here for you. But you can always start again by turning to Chapter 1.

The excitement has caused even more of a stir outside the hotel. You're aware that things are starting to heat up. And while the attention may have prevented you from being strangled or beaten up at the hands of Toothpick and Boffi, it's not exactly the easiest environment to solve a murder case.

You excuse yourself from the scene and hurry back inside the Royale Premiere. Everything Camilla Boffi told you about Peter von Hiltz is racing through your mind. You can't trust a gangster's moll, can you? She wanted you off Mr Walter's case, no doubt because she wanted her money. And if the hotel manager testifies or makes a plea bargain, her whole empire might come crashing down around your ears.

But that's for another day's worry. Right now your hands are full with the murder of Blanche Aikerman. Camilla Boffi is a mercenary, cold and calculated, the brains behind the whole Boffi operation, if she's to be believed. The fact that she moves in such high circles in Hollywood is a perfect cover. In fact, having met her you can't think of a *better* place to hide than with the fakes and phonies of Tinseltown's elite.

She seemed genuine enough about Blanche's murder. The fact that she *knew* about the tragedy long before everyone else suggests that she has nothing to do with it. Not directly at least. And then you come back to Peter von Hiltz. Boffi named him specifically, saying that he should be examined. The director has been elusive since you first arrived on the scene. You've had neither sight nor sound of him. For someone who is as prominent in this business and who worked so closely with Blanche, that strikes you as odd.

Perhaps there is something in this von Hiltz line of enquiry after all. Perhaps it's time you spoke with him directly to see what he thinks of everything that's gone on. You head over to the main reception desk. There's no use trying to find him among this miasma of people. The Royale Premiere is gearing up for the biggest night in the entertainment industry's calendar. With every passing moment, more and more stars are flooding in through the entranceway. You decide to ask the reception staff to put out a call for von Hiltz. Make him come to you, that's the sensible approach. And sensibility has been sorely lacking in this world for a long while.

A friendly staff member greets you with a large smile. You're about to ask her for help when she holds up a telephone.

'It's a call for you, officer,' she says. 'Your squad room – it's urgent.'

You take the urgent call on page 70.

'Oh, come on, officer,' she laughs. 'You're seriously trying to tell me you think I don't know what's going on in this sleazy little town? Look at me, I'm the wife of The Hammer. Any murder, extortion, arson, fraud or card racket that's running in LA is my daily business. Sure, my man likes to think he's the brains of the operation but the poor dear can barely count. No, no, anything that happens on the darker side of the law in this city comes through *me* and me only. I swear, my life would make a great movie. Only the suits and ties that run these things aren't interested in me. A little too trashy, they say, when I'm not around. Rich coming from them when they're up to their necks in debt to my husband and use my brothels every other weekend. But hey, that's how it works, right? Who am I to complain?'

Toothpick and Scar laugh a little. Boffi flashes a beautiful smile at you. It's all false, augmented, she's been under the surgeon's knife, you can tell. But that doesn't really matter. There's a charm to her. And the brutal honesty she's showing to a LAPD homicide detective is weirdly refreshing.

'Do you know who's responsible?' she asks.

You say that you're here on confidential business. And that the investigations of the LAPD homicide unit are not of the concern of a public citizen.

'That's a very polite way of telling me to take a walk, am I right, officer?'

She turns and stalks off towards the opposite side of the stage. You feel Toothpick and Scar nudge you in the back to follow. Boffi glides down the steps and onto the main floor. You are close behind, the heavies leaving a little distance between you.

Boffi starts up the central aisle. Her hand dances from one velvet seat to the next, casually bouncing as she tilts her head back towards you.

'I always wanted to be an actress, you know,' she says. 'When I was a little girl, growing up in Brooklyn, it was all I wanted. I used to sneak into the movies with my brothers. I never knew what the credits were until I was a teenager. We always got thrown out long before the movie finished. But I loved it all the same. The magic of the cinema, telling stories, and the stars of course. They were all so glamorous. My favourite was Elizabeth Gresham. She was beautiful, drop-dead gorgeous. And legs that stretched from the ground all the way up to heaven. I never got the chance to act, to learn. Life was tough for my family, no money, no luck. Then I met Silvio. We were too young to marry but we did it anyway. Ten years later and we're out here on the coast where it's sunny all the time and they can't make ragù to save their lives. I was too old to learn how to act so I did the next best thing. I bribed my way behind the scenes and now I'm one of the patrons. Can you believe that? A little hoodlum from Brooklyn deciding who gets a Golden Star. Funny how the world works, eh?'

She's made her way to the top of the aisle. The doors to the main lobby are behind her. She spins around, dramatically and leans on the end seat of the last row. Everything Camilla Boffi does is effortless. You believe she could make changing a tyre something spectacular to behold.

'This business with Blanche Aikerman, I want you to know I had nothing to do with it,' she says flatly. 'Whacking film stars, especially the biggest ones on the planet, that ain't my style. I didn't know the girl, never spoke to her. She didn't owe my husband any money, she didn't put her nose into where it didn't belong. She was clean, as far as I knew. And I had no grudge. Now, your Mr Walter, he's a different case altogether.'

A darkness seems to fall over Boffi. And for the first time you get the sense that this woman is indeed the powerful underworld figure you've only heard rumours about.

'We govern ourselves, detective,' she says, walking slowly towards you. 'Everything that's in the light, that's for the LAPD. You've got your hands full here, with Blanche Aikerman's murder. The absolute *last* thing you need is to be dipping your toe in the business affairs of me and my husband. I don't doubt for a second that you're a good cop, I can smell it off you.'

She leans in close to you and sniffs the air. Her hypnotic eyes look you up and down. She smells of expensive perfume, a pleasant change from Toothpick's breath.

'I won't try to insult your IQ by offering you a bribe. Just a little bit of friendly, free advice,' she says. 'Walter's business with me and The Hammer is just that. Between me and The Hammer. He's not your killer. I'm not an alibi or anything but I know the man. He's a gambler, a loser, one of life's hard-luck cases who wallows in his own misery. That said, he's not capable of killing anyone, let alone Blanche Aikerman. You're barking up the wrong tree if you think that's the case, detective. And I think you're smarter than that.'

She runs the back of her hand against your cheek, tracing your chin with her finger, tipped with blood-red nails to match her lips.

You ask Boffi if she's so confident that Walter isn't the killer, does she know who murdered Blanche Aikerman.

Boffi laughs. She walks past you, brushing her bare arm against yours.

'You've got balls, I'll give you that, detective,' she throws a gaze back over her shoulder. 'Asking a lady if she knows who killed a young woman, on the eve of the Goldies. It takes some guts to be that forthright.'

Boffi walks back down the central aisle until she reaches the stage. Toothpick and Scar are waiting for her, towering over her from the stage like a pair of granite statues. She hops up onto the edge of the stage and lifts her arms into the air. Like something from a hit musical or Broadway show, the heavies lift her and place her down between them. Her gaze never leaves you as you expect a big band to kick in at any moment.

'What do you know about Victor Ramsay?' she asks you.

You shake your head. The name sounds vaguely familiar.

'He's a big cheese at Thundersaga Pictures,' says Boffi, taking a cigarette from Scar. 'That's where Blanche did most of her work. Her *good* work at least.'

Toothpick lights the cigarette for Boffi as it hangs from her lips.

'You might want to take a look at his background a little, he was in the army you know,' she says. 'Used to killing, that sort of thing. Maybe he knows the ins and outs of what Blanche was going through. I dunno. Just a little friendly advice. Use it as you wish.'

She blows out a puff of smoke and winks at you.

'See you around, detective,' she says, before turning her back on you and walking towards the back of the stage.

That was not your best move and you're still not sure on who killed Blanche Aikerman. What now?

- You head down to the lobby to hunt out Victor Ramsay of

  Thundersaga Pictures on page 62

- You return to the main lobby on the next page

This case is growing more and more complicated with every turn. You need a moment to think, to straighten out everything that's happened in the last little while. There's also the small matter of examining the crime scene more thoroughly. However, you're aware of how busy things are getting in the lobby of the Royale Premiere. The more time marches on, the more people will arrive at the venue. And that means press, reporters, cameramen and photographers.

The last thing you need is a mass panic on your hands if word gets out there's a killer on the loose. You head over to the reception desk. A young woman behind the long, marble counter waves over to you as soon as you arrive.

'Officer, it's your squad room, an urgent call,' she says.

- Ignore the call and turn to page 179 police badge icon
- You take the call on page 70 police badge icon

You thank the receptionist for alerting you but you decline to take the call. You have a feeling you know who it is – Captain Barclay. He's the head of the LAPD homicide unit and your boss. There will be demands for you to get back to the station – it's a busy weekend here after all. But you can't leave, not yet. Not with Blanche's body still lying upstairs.

You think about calling in the lab techs and some back-up. But while the tragedy is still under wraps, you stand a chance of catching the killer. Surprise is your best weapon. And in a murder investigation, you'll take every advantage you're given.

You scan the lobby of the Royale Premiere. The place is still busy, if anything it's actually getting *busier* than before. The whole hotel feels like it's a seething cauldron of activity. From journalists sniffing out stories to the great and the good of Hollywood waltzing around hoping to be spotted. They don't care by who. Anyone will do. From the all-too brief dalliances you've had with the celebrities that populate Tinseltown, there's nothing they love more than themselves.

There's a young couple, actors by the look of their clothes, over by the main entranceway. They're posing together, embracing each other for a crowd of baying photographers. They kiss and smile, smile and kiss, over and over again. You vaguely recognise them from some romp or romantic flick that was released last year. Showbusiness types always seem to be living their lives in the public domain. Nothing ever seems private. The only privacy that Blanche Aikerman has received is the anonymity of her murder. But even that won't last forever.

That gets you thinking about something Victor Ramsay just said. He mentioned that he didn't get involved with his employees' personal lives. Something about that statement just doesn't ring true to your mind. Surely somebody in his position, the head of one of the most successful film studios in Hollywood, would want, *need* to know what his workers were up to. Knowing is half the battle when it comes to publicity and managing scandals. You've read enough cheap showbiz rags and tawdry, rumour columns to know that these actors are always up to no good. The idea that someone as powerful as Victor Ramsay *doesn't* know what his stars are getting up to seems ludicrous. And if he's lying about that, what else is he lying about?

You decide you need to question him further. You search through the miasma of people in the main foyer of the Royale Premiere. Somebody as huge and imposing as Victor Ramsay can't be difficult to lose. He stands out like a giant sore thumb everywhere he goes. And yet there's no sign of him. He's vanished. This can't be a coincidence. A powerful movie mogul disappears a matter of moments after learning of Blanche Aikerman's death.

How do you want to proceed?

- You ask reception what room Ramsay is staying in and head for there on page 183

- You try to find Victor Ramsay by foot, searching the hotel on the next page

With the lobby as busy as it is, you make your way to the back of the area. You begin to search the adjoining annexes that lead to the different parts of the wider Royale Premiere resort. You start with the bar directly across from reception.

The place is full. Every table and booth is taken up. Conversations are flowing back and forth, a hubbub rising above punctuated only by occasional laughter or breaking glass. You recognise some of the faces here, from the magazines and newspapers. Everywhere you turn there's somebody famous. Old, young, new, legend. The Golden Star Awards really brings out the great and the good of Hollywood.

None of that interests you at the moment. You're not hunting autographs here, after all. You're conducting a murder investigation and you need to find Victor Ramsay. There's no sign of him here in the bar. You give up and march back out into the main lobby and on to the next annexe.

The spa of the hotel is a little more closed off. There's a small reception desk at the front before guests are invited into the back for facials, massages and manicures – nothing too luxurious for Goldies guests. It feels like a longshot. Ramsay doesn't strike you as the kind of person who would get his nails painted. But you ask at the front desk if he's been seen.

'I'm afraid not, officer,' says the pleasant attendee. 'I know Mr Ramsay, he often stays at the hotel but I've not seen him since breakfast this morning. Or was it yesterday morning, I can't quite recall. He's not the kind of person you miss, if you know what I mean.'

You thank her for her help and move on. You spot a sign that points in the direction of the pool terrace. It's worth a shot.

Heading outside, the warm afternoon air washes over you, followed quickly by the sickly scent of something more exotic. A good-looking couple are close to the door. When the man, his eyes covered by expensive shades, spots you, he quickly pulls something from his mouth, crushes it out under his shiny shoes and wafts away the smoke. You've got more important things on your mind than to collar a perp for smoking a jazz cigarette, so you ignore it. The couple look anxious, pained smiles across their faces as you walk past them. It's never occurred to you before but the fact you're a cop must ooze out of you, like the bright lights of the Hollywood sign at night.

A large pool dominates the terrace. The paving stones around are bleached white with the sun and chlorine. There are plenty of sun-loungers dotted about the terrace but nobody is catching any rays. They are too busy, too deep, in conversations, like their colleagues back in the bar. Again, there's no sign of Victor Ramsay. You curse under your breath and head back inside the hotel.

It's starting to dawn on you that there's a good chance you've lost him. He could be anywhere by now, while you've been searching. If he *is* still in the hotel, then there's no telling what direction he went in after he left you and you dallied. Worst-case scenario; he's left the complex altogether and could be heading anywhere in Los Angeles. Or beyond. A man like Victor Ramsay has means and resources to get out of the city quickly if he chooses.

There's a sinking inevitability that you're not going to find him. You thump your fist into your open palm and walk slowly back to the reception area. The young woman who called you over before spots you and waves again.

'Sorry to bother you again, officer, but it's another call from your captain,' she says. 'He wants to speak with you urgently.'

This sounds bad. You take the call on page 70.

'Mr Ramsay is staying in one of our villas,' says the friendly receptionist at the front desk. 'We have a number of very small, private dwellings beyond the pool area, just at the rear of the hotel. He's staying in the largest one, Villa Twenty.'

You thank her for her help and information. Following the signs, you move through the crowds of the hotel. You feel like a ghost, a spirit, somebody who isn't really there. This is a world you know nothing about. Showbusiness is a world that *most* people know nothing about. It's closed off to the general public, both deliberately and accidentally. The movie-going punters don't want to think their screen heroes can die, let alone be murdered like Blanche Aikerman. She's not supposed to be mortal. Not like them. She should glow and shine, stand above all others like a Goddess from the Greek Myths. Instead she's upstairs, covered in blood, her life long expired. And it's your job to catch the culprit who did that to her.

You wonder, as you weave and duck through the assembled guests, staff and media, if anybody would really care about what's happened to Blanche. From the brief introduction you've had to this world, nothing ever appears as it seems. There's always an ulterior motive, an angle. And that usually means somebody stands to gain.

In that respect, is any of this any different to any other murder you've ever investigated? Whether it's for money, revenge or even love, the taking of somebody's life always boils down to the haves and the have-nots. This time, it seems, it's just of a grander, more glamorous and glitzy scale. But murder is murder. And it's your job to bring the killer to justice.

The heaving mass of humanity slowly begins to peter out as you near the back of the main lobby and entrance of the Royale Premiere. You climb the stairs and push through a set of double doors, emerging on a sun-drenched deck where the pool is located. This place is much quieter. There are a few guests dotted around the pool on sun loungers, catching the fading afternoon rays of another warm day in Los Angeles. You skip quickly across the terrace and through a gate. A path winds its way through what looks like a large garden area. Tall palm trees snuff out the sunlight and there's a coolness to this place that's quite comfortable. Exotic plants and shrubs sprout out from the grass and undergrowth on either side of the path.

Up ahead you spot the villas the receptionist described. They're small, squat little buildings with tiled terracotta roofs. Nothing elaborate or fancy, not like the Royale Premiere. Seclusion away from the crowds is the name of the game here. And you can understand why somebody like Victor Ramsay would choose to stay in this part of the resort.

Counting up the numbers as you pass each building, you eventually come to Villa Twenty. The front door is closed, the windows dark. You follow the path and knock on the door. There's no answer. You try again. Still no answer.

If he isn't coming to you, what's next?

- You increase your search of him in the hotel on the next

  page

- Try another way into the villa on page 186

You give the door a knock once more, hoping that Victor Ramsay will answer. There's still nothing from the other side. There's a chance, of course, that the studio executive hasn't returned to his quarters. And that you might still catch up with him at some point. You also acknowledge that there are strong odds that he's skipped the hotel altogether. And is currently gunning his way down to Mexico, never to be seen again.

You retreat from the villa and head back up towards the pool deck. More glamorous guests have filtered out and are catching the last of the sun. The sound of cocktail shakers drifts through the air, mingling with all the fake laughter and quiet conversations that are taking place amongst the gathered glitterati.

You head back into the main lobby and head for the reception desk. There's still no sign of Victor Ramsay anywhere and you begin to suspect he's completely gone. Trying to catch up with him now seems like an impossibility. The implications weigh heavy on your mind.

The kindly receptionist smiles and flags you down as you near the desk. She's holding up a phone.

'Another call for you, officer,' she says. 'It's a Captain Barclay, he wants to speak with you urgently. He's called at least three times since I last told you.'

Resigned to getting a stern lecture from your superior officer, you
decide to take the call on page 70.

Making sure nobody is about, you round the side of the villa. The bushes and plants are overgrown this far down into the estate. Pushing through the undergrowth, you find that the back garden of the villa is walled off. It's not that tall and you slowly climb up and over.

Dropping down onto the other side, a small courtyard opens up behind the main building. There's a pool, although for a man of Victor Ramsay's size, it would probably only feel like a bathtub. A small table with two chairs and a huge sun umbrella are near a set of patio doors that lead into the villa. It's dark inside and there's no sign of movement let alone life.

You try the patio doors. It's surprising how many people leave doors unlocked in this city. You often wonder that if the good people of Los Angeles were a little more paranoid, you wouldn't ever be so busy. This is another example of that odd trusting complex the City of Angels has developed. The glass door opens easily and you step inside. It's cool, almost cold, inside, and there's a musky smell about the place.

You shout out, calling out Victor Ramsay's name. There's no answer. Everything seems to be in order, at least on first inspection. The furniture is all in place. There are no stray dishes or cutlery and glasses strewn about. Even the complimentary magazines are stacked neatly on the coffee table in the middle of the living room. And that's what bothers you.

None of the villa appears lived-in. Even if the housekeeping staff had been in, there would be little signs here and there that Victor Ramsay had at least spent a night here. Instead, it all seems too pristine, too perfect. You check the bedroom – the bed neatly made, side tables clear and empty. There are no personal items in here, no toothbrush, no shampoo, nothing. You're starting to wonder if you have the wrong villa. Or that the receptionist has got things wrong.

Then you hear something from outside. The front door clicks open. Victor Ramsay's unmistakable voice drifts into the bedroom. You hurry over to the door and stay out of sight.

Ramsay's huge bulk passes the door. It's followed by another figure, but you can't quite make out who it is. They head to the kitchen area that overlooks the main living room. Ramsay opens the door of the refrigerator.

'I think this calls for a celebration, don't you?' he laughs.

He reaches in and pulls out a bottle. Popping the cork, it's clear that he has champagne. Finding two flutes from a cupboard, he pours and clinks with the stranger.

'I must say, this isn't how I thought today was going to turn out. Or the awards season for that matter,' says Ramsay, draining his glass. 'Just when you think you've figured this business out, something comes along and completely pulls the rug from under your feet. It's remarkable really. You get taught in the army, I don't know if you served, to expect the unexpected. I can't say that's at all true here in Hollywood. The opposite in fact.'

You crane to try and see who Ramsay is with. It's dark out there, the sunlight fading. They have their back turned to you and they haven't said anything yet. All you can see is that they are tall, slender, wearing a long, dark trench coat of some kind. The longer you wait, the greater the chance of being discovered.

'Blanche Aikerman will be missed, sure,' Ramsay goes on. 'But there will be another pretty face like hers to fill her place in the next six months. And as for the box office, I can't even begin to imagine what her movies will make when this news gets out. We could be looking at a record year, on top of everything we've made this year. Wonderful stuff. It's all worked out well in the end.'

He laughs again. This is a very different Victor Ramsay to the one you spoke with in the lobby of the Royale Premiere. He pours another glass from the champagne bottle and drains it in one gulp.

Your back is straining, leaning against the wall, trying not to be detected. You try to see who Ramsay is speaking with. You overstretch and your hand slips off the handle of the door. You fall forward, into the room, landing hard on the carpet. In a panic, you scramble to your feet. Victor Ramsay is standing perfectly still, bottle of champagne still in his hand. His face goes slack when he realises who you are.

Before you can react, the stranger with Ramsay takes off. You still can't see who they are as they bolt for the door. Everything happens in a heartbeat. Ramsay bolts as fast as his huge bulk will allow, running towards the patio doors in the opposite direction. You can only follow one of them.

- Ramsay? (Go to page 197)

- The stranger? (Go to page 189)

Whoever they are, they're fast. You thought your days of running after perps were long gone. That's the job of the uniforms. They're fitter, not to mention faster. Too many afternoons guzzling coffee and sucking jam doughnuts has left you slower than you used to be.

You press on, hurrying back up the pathway, between the flopping palm trees and buzzing undergrowth. You burst through the gate and back out onto the pool terrace, the mighty Royale Premiere looming overhead.

Your sudden appearance on the pool terrace seems to have attracted some attention. Designer sunglasses are tipped forward, polite chatter abruptly stops. You straighten, adjusting your collar and coat. It's strangely unnerving to have Hollywood's great and good all staring at you. Their interest, thankfully, doesn't last long and they quickly go back to their conversations and libations.

That unpleasantness aside, you look about the terrace for the stranger in the long coat. Nothing seems odd or out of place. There's a good chance that you've missed them. They had a headstart after all. And they could be anywhere by now, in the hotel, out on the street, anywhere.

You take a deep breath and try to get your thoughts in order. Out of the corner of your eye you spot Mr Walter, the hotel manager. He's sitting at a small table close to the edge of the pool terrace, a tall, empty glass and a newspaper in front of him. He spots you and waves over. You go to join him.

'Good grief,' he says. 'You look rather flushed, officer. Is anything the matter?'

You pull out another chair from the table and sit down. It's nice to get off your feet. It feels like you've been pounding the beat for a century. You let out a deep breath and rub your forehead. The case is starting to get to you, you can feel it. The weight of expectation, the Herculean task of keeping everything under wraps, it's all starting to strain. You ask Mr Walter if he saw anyone in a long black coat come running through here. He is, as expected, unhelpful.

'No, I can't say I did,' he says. 'I'm just taking a quick break. It's been a monumental day, not that I have to tell you that, officer. The Golden Star Awards are always a chore. But with, well, everything that's happened to Blanche Aikerman, it's all become something of a nuisance.'

You nod in agreement.

'Can I assume you are no further forward in your investigation?' he asks.

You say that's not exactly the case. You're making progress but you still have no idea who might have murdered Blanche.

'Such a terrible pity,' he says. 'Blanche was a wonderful girl, so beautiful, so talented. I can't begin to imagine what everyone will think or say when they find out what's happened to her. I haven't been able to find Mr von Hiltz at all. And the owners of the hotel are on vacation in the Bahamas at the moment. It will hit the fan, to use the parlance of our times. Utterly tragic.'

You nod in agreement again. Your head begins to hurt, it's throbbing. Blanche's murder, the suspects, losing the stranger and now Victor Ramsay. Everything feels like it's coming apart. Mr Walter reaches into his pocket and produces a packet of cigarettes, Chesterfields, and offers you one.

You tell him you don't smoke. He pops a cigarette into his mouth and returns the packet to the inside of his smart suit jacket. Patting himself, he tries to find his lighter. Only then do you spot something, something a little odd. A bead of sweat is running down Walter's right temple. There are more on his forehead, just below his black and silver hair swept back with the help of a hefty dollop of pomade.

The hotel manager seems to realise something. He stops patting his pockets with a sudden urgency, like he's just remembered where his lighter is. You sit up, look at him across the table. He doesn't meet your gaze, fidgeting, uncomfortable.

You lean over the side of your chair, looking beneath the table between you both. Across from you, under Mr Walter, you spot that he's sitting on something. A long, black sleeve drops out from beneath him as he fidgets. You realise that *he* is the stranger you've been searching for.

'I can explain,' says Walter, nervously.

Suddenly, he pushes the table forward. It digs into your ribs and knocks the breath from you for a moment. The hotel manager vaults out of his chair and begins to run. This time you're quicker. You push through the pain, free yourself from the table and give chase. Walter bolts across the terrace, cigarettes flying from his jacket. You're faster now that you can see him. You pump your legs like the pistons of a great steam ship, motoring after the manager of the Royale Premiere.

When he's close enough, you leap with all of your might. You tackle Walter, but your momentum carries you both forward. The stone terrace vanishes from beneath your feet and you crash into the pool with an almighty splash.

The roar of the bubbles fills your ears. You hold your breath, Walter struggling beside you, above you, everywhere. You aim a fist somewhere into the movement and he seems to relax. Then you kick your legs and the breathable world comes rushing back.

'I … I can't swim!' Walter wimpers beside you.

You grab him by the collar and swim both of you towards the edge of the pool. A small crowd has gathered on the edge and they help him onto the terrace. He's coughing, spluttering, gasping for breath as you climb out beside him. Drenched, you lean down and help him to his feet, explaining to the crowd that this is police business. You march Walter over towards the entrance of the hotel, every set of eyes watching you both as you go.

Inside is much quieter. You find an empty hallway and shove Walter in front of you. Your feet squelch in your shoes, two sets of wet footprints soaking the expensive carpet as you both get away and out of sight. At the end of the hallway is a small sofa. You shove Walter down and he cowers, holding his hands up.

'Please … please don't hurt me,' he says.

What's next officer?

- You haul him out of the pool and put your handcuff on him on

  page 192

- You haul him out of the pool and interrogate him on

  page 193

'Please, please I'm begging you,' says Walter. 'This will leave my reputation in tatters. I'll be fired. I haven't done anything wrong. This industry, this job, it makes things very difficult. You can't just say "no" to these people, they're powerful, they control the financial fate of a hotel like this. I was only doing what Mr Ramsay asked of me. He wanted to know everything that was going on with Blanche Aikerman while she stayed here. Who she saw, what she ate, everything. That's all I was doing. I shouldn't have lied to you, or ran. I panicked, that's all. Please, I'm begging you detective, don't do this.'

You ignore Walter's pleas and march him through the lobby of the hotel. There are a few gasps as you pass some of the guests and staff. Nobody dares get in your way. You reach the main reception area and bundle him behind the main desk. The friendly receptionist from earlier spots you both. She's a little speechless, then she remembers where she is and snaps back into action. She picks up a receiver and hands it to you.

'A call for you, detective,' she says. 'It's your captain from the squad room, he says it's urgent.'

Your first stroke of luck. You were going to call for back-up anyway. Turn to page 70.

'I'm … I'm sorry, I don't know what I was thinking of running away like that. I'm sorry, please don't arrest me,' he says.

You tell him he needs to start giving you answers quickly, otherwise you're hauling him down to the station in cuffs.

'No, no, no, please, you can't do that to me,' he says. 'My reputation will be ruined if I'm arrested. I'll lose my job, my pension. Taking a tumble into the pool in front of all those guests is bad enough. I couldn't possibly live down being arrested.'

You explain to him again, slowly, that he needs to start giving you some answers. You tell him that you were in the villa when he was there speaking with Ramsay. And how the executive seemed to be cosying up to him over something – something involving Blanche Aikerman's death. At the mention of the dead actress, Walter's bottom lip begins to tremble.

'It's such a terrible mess,' he says, planting his face in his hands. 'All of this, it couldn't have come at a worse time. This weekend, the awards, everything surrounding Blanche. Why did I have to get involved like this?'

You pull Walter's hands free. You tell him that you're seconds away from arresting him.

'You have to understand, my role here at the Royale Premiere, it's not just as simple as being the manager. I'm the conduit for these stars, these film people, and the real world,' he says. 'The things they get up to, behind closed doors, it would make your teeth itch. Honestly, detective, if you had a spare decade I could bring you up to speed on just the last twelve months alone. Trashed suites, parties that go on for days, weeks on end, it's endless. And that's just the well-behaved ones. Some of the celebrities that walk through our doors don't know what day of the week it is, let alone where they are staying. It's my job, as hotel manager, to make sure the Royale Premiere's reputation remains intact throughout all of these shenanigans. And that none of this ever makes it to the press.'

Walter suddenly looks ten years older. The wrinkles on his forehead have deepened, his eyes burrowed into his skull. His pencil moustache is drooping over his top lip.

'The actors are the worst, as you can imagine,' he says. 'But it's a different beast dealing with the directors, the producers, the executives like Victor Ramsay. They're the money, detective, but they're just as removed from reality as the stars. It's up to me and my staff to bridge that gap, between reality and fantasy. We are practical, discreet, and professional at all costs. That's why this issue with Blanche Aikerman has been so difficult. She was so famous, perhaps the most famous guest we've ever had, certainly under my watch. As such, I've had all kinds of bizarre requests, especially since her untimely demise.'

You ask who from.

'Mr Ramsay, for one,' he says. 'That's why I was meeting with him in his villa. The champagne was perhaps a little overkill, if I can say that. He wanted me to keep him abreast of everything that was going on with Blanche. To spy on her for him. Much like Mr von Hiltz too. They both wanted information on Blanche. Whether the other knew what they were up to, I'm never really sure. They're powerful men, detective, they're not the kind of people you want to say "no" to. So that's what I did. I kept them in the loop about the murder, about what you've been doing. Although I haven't seen Mr von Hiltz in hours now. I'm sorry.'

Walter has done nothing illegal. You found it hard to believe that there wasn't some sort of seedy spy network operating out of sight. Keeping the murder of Blanche Aikerman a secret is like holding back the tide. An impossible task, even for the best in the business. You remind Walter that this is a murder investigation and that a killer is still on the loose.

'I know, I'm truly sorry,' he says. 'From now on, everything I know and everything you tell me will be kept firmly in confidence.'

You nod. There's nothing to make you think that Walter is lying. It's become glaringly obvious throughout your time in this world that nothing is ever as it first seems. Smoke and mirrors are the order of the day. You tell Walter that he's free to go but to make sure nobody goes anywhere near the crime scene unless you are notified first.

'Thank you, detective, thank you, thank you,' he says.

He motions to hug you but thinks better of it. The hotel manager slinks away down the corridor, his figurative tail firmly between his legs.

You can head back to the reception area on the next page or try your luck at Ramsay's villa again on page 197.
How you progress your investigation is up to you.

Things are getting busy here. There are more than a few cocked eyebrows as you walk through the crowd, your feet still squelching in your shoes from the unplanned dip in the pool.

Before you plot your next move, the friendly receptionist from earlier waves you down. She has the phone in her hand.

'A call for you, detective,' she says. 'It's your captain from the squad room, he says it's urgent.'

You take the call on page 70.

The studio executive doesn't bother with the patio doors. He barrels through them, sending glass everywhere. Ramsay doesn't miss a step, stumbling onto the little terrace behind the villa. You follow close behind, carefully ducking through the shattered glass of the patio doors.

Ramsay has crossed the courtyard. You speed up. He makes an attempt to leap up the wall but his bulk is too heavy. He crashes down hard and you swear you could feel the ground rumble beneath your feet. As you approach, he spots you and spins. The bottle of champagne is still in his hands. He swings it wildly, almost catching you on the side of the face.

He swings again. This time you duck. The swing carries around in a large arc and the bottle smashes off the wall. Champagne sprays into your eyes and you're dazed for a second. You wipe your eyes just in time to see Ramsay coming at you again. He waves the broken champagne bottle in front of you, its edges sharp.

'You shouldn't be here,' rasps Ramsay. 'This is private property!'

He swings wildly at you. You back away, trying to anticipate his next move. For a man as big as he is, the studio executive is fast. Then you remember what he told you earlier, about being in the military. You realise that this could go horribly wrong if you give him half a chance.

He lunges forward, trying to stab you. You manage to parry the blow and step to the side. Using Ramsay's weight against him, you hurl him forward. He trips and smashes head first into the wall of the villa. Groaning, he lies still for a moment while you catch your breath.

Ramsay rolls over. There's a large gash on his forehead. He's still holding the broken champagne bottle but his grip has loosened. You kick it away from him and produce your handcuffs. The bracelet barely makes it around the executive's thick wrists. You chain him to the drain pipe that runs up the side wall of the villa, although you suspect a strong breeze could probably break him free.

Making sure Ramsay is in no immediate danger of expiring, you hand him your handkerchief. He wipes the blood from his forehead with his free hand and just sits there. He's like an elephant, tired from the chase, massive suit creased and covered in dirt.

'I guess you're wondering why I ran, officer,' he says, voice hoarse. 'What can I say? I have a pathological fear of authority figures.'

He slowly catches his breath. The cut on his forehead is starting to bruise and swell. You know you should get him some medical treatment. But time is pressing. And you suspect he knows more about Blanche Aikerman's murder than he let you know before. There's also the small matter of the stranger who bolted from the villa when you crashed the party.

- Ramsay's hurt and will need some medical attention. Turn to page 199 to make sure the LAPD still has a perp

  to talk to

- Injured or not, Ramsay knows something. You ask what he

  knows about the stranger on page 200

The friendly receptionist's smile from earlier quickly drops when you say you need a doctor or an ambulance. She begins to flap a little, ruffling paperwork as she tries to think. You tell her not to panic, but Mr Ramsay has had an accident and needs checking over.

'Yes, of course, I'll call for an ambulance,' she says. 'Is he at his villa?'

You say he is and that he's currently handcuffed to a drain pipe. Her eyes widen. You say it's just routine, while you conduct your investigations. That seems to jog a memory and she clicks her fingers.

'You have a call waiting for you, detective,' she says, finding a scrap of paper by a phone. 'A Captain Barclay wants you to call him straight away, he says that it's urgent.'

The captain is calling, I'll have to take this. Turn to page 70.

'You're going to have to get me a doctor,' he says. 'A scratch like this, it could turn septic. I saw it during the war, men losing their legs, their arms, after getting nothing more than a papercut. You wouldn't want something like this to turn out like that, would you, officer?'

He points at the gash on his forehead. You're not convinced but assure him he'll get the help he needs, once he's answered a few questions. Ramsay laughs.

'You're a professional, I'll give you that,' he says.

He leans to one side. For a moment, you think he might be having a turn. But he remains conscious, determined, as he pulls something out of the back pocket of his giant trousers and throws it over to you before sitting back. He rests his head against the villa wall.

'Open it,' he says. 'It's my pocket book.'

The wallet has landed at your feet. You pick it up and look back at the studio executive.

'There's two thousand dollars in there, cash,' he says. 'Help yourself.'

You leaf through the perfectly crisp notes that are stacked in the pocket book.

'I'm not a patient man, I don't have the time. I assume you heard everything I said in there so I don't want this getting out. Take the money, officer, don't be stupid. I'll wager that's more than you've made this quarter. All for turning a blind eye. That, and letting me go, of course.'

- Take the cash on page 201
- Say that you can't be bought on page 203

The chief of Thundersaga Pictures stands up. He rubs his wrist where the bracelet was digging into the skin. Nodding at you, he smiles.

'Glad you saw sense, officer,' he said. 'I like a professional who knows a good deal when they see one. Believe me, this is a good deal. I wouldn't want what went on in there to be construed as anything unsavoury. You see, Blanche Aikerman, put simply, she just had to die.'

You look at the huge man towering over you. Ramsay is leering, a madness in his eyes. You ask him, bluntly, if he was the one who cut Blanche's throat. He laughs, that unmistakable, bellowing laugh of his.

'Of course I didn't,' he said. 'I wouldn't get my hands dirty with something like that. Too much of a risk. That's why that nice Mr Walter, you saw him chatting to me, that's why he did the needful for me.'

He throws a huge arm around your shoulder and guides you back into the villa. Broken glass crunches beneath your feet from the obliterated patio doors.

'You see, a star like Blanche Aikerman, they burn brightly but they burn quickly, too. You get five, maybe ten years tops out of these actors before you have to start searching for the next big thing. It was the same before Blanche. Nobody is talking about Elizabeth Gresham anymore, are they? She's forgotten, long forgotten, greying away in her palace of memories while the world moves on. We've been very lucky at Thundersaga, we've had some of the greats grace our sound stages. It's exhausting, officer, really it is. I've been in this industry a very long time and when you build somebody up, make them a hero to millions around the globe, it takes it out of you. I'm getting older, of course I am, and I don't have the same energy as I used to. That's why Blanche had to die. You see, a star that fades is no use to this industry, or me. But one who is snuffed out in her prime, well, she'll live forever. And so will the returns at the box office.'

You feel the sickness rising in the back of your throat. Listening to Ramsay speak so casually about Blanche and showbusiness in such a callous, cold manner makes you want to retch. Even more so now that you're in his pocket after taking the bribe.

'It's just one of the many facts of life we all have to come to terms with, I'm afraid,' says Ramsay. 'Like the fact I can't let you simply walk out of here knowing what you know.'

Before you can fully react to what he just said, Ramsay wraps his big arms around you in a bear hug. He's strong, stronger than you ever thought possible. He hauls you off your feet and tightens his grip. You feel the air being squeezed out of you, like a tube of toothpaste. You try to resist but there's no use. His arms are thicker than the trunks of oak trees and his grip is like a vice.

The energy is sapping from you as you try to thrash and kick out. Nothing is going to break the grip.

'I'm sorry, officer,' he says, teeth gritted, veins bulging in his neck and forehead. 'But it's for your own good. When your colleagues arrive, they'll find you and assume that Aikerman's murderer got to you when you were sticking your nose where it shouldn't. Or there's a chance you've been snuffed out by the mob, a jealous star, take your pick, it doesn't matter to me. I'll be more than happy to help out with their investigations, naturally. After all, I'm a respected citizen of this town.'

He tightens his grip one last time. You make one final, feeble attempt to break free but it's no use. You feel your ribs cracking as he chokes the very life from you. Everything starts to turn dark and you go limp.

Taking a bribe from a suspect was the wrong decision, even if you had the best of intentions. If you stand firm against the intimidating mogul on page 203, you might find that Ramsay can prove to be a valuable source for your inquiries.

Ramsay laughs bitterly. Then he nods.

'I thought so,' he says. 'Good, principled cops are hard to come by these days. You're something of an anomaly. Not that I need to tell you that. I'm sure you know all about your colleagues' extracurricular activities when it comes to organised crime and shakedowns of the man on the street. Yes, I know all about the bent streak that runs through the LAPD. How the hell do you think so many of my stars and directors, producers even, are still walking the streets when they should be locked up in San Quentin rotting away with the rest of the scum. Hollywood, my dear officer, is a stinking cesspit of greed and lies. Except for you, it seems.'

You tell Ramsay that if he thinks flattery will get him out of this, he's very much mistaken. That draws a laugh from the studio executive. He looks at you with a genuine smile.

'My dear detective, if I thought you could actually be bought off I would have offered you double what's in my pocket book. No, you're a breath of fresh air. We could have been doing with more like you in the army, when we were up to our necks in mud trying to kill Nazis.'

He shifts uncomfortably again. A thin streak of blood runs from the gash on his forehead. He wipes it with your handkerchief. You ask him who he was talking to back inside the villa.

'I may be a lot of things,' he says. 'But, one thing I'm not, is a snitch.'

You remind him that you're a homicide detective, investigating the murder of Blanche Aikerman. And if he doesn't start talking you've got very good reason to haul him down to the station and let the lawyers take their shots.

'Okay, all right,' he says, trying to calm you down. 'I know what this looks like. And yes, I can also understand that what you might have heard in there could be construed as my confession into murdering Blanche. But I want you to understand that it's not like that, not like that at all. I never harmed a hair on her head. Sure, now that she's gone, the studio is going to make a fortune from her old films. I'm not going to lie to you and say that doesn't make me at least a little bit happy. A tragedy, sure, but this is showbusiness and you're only as good as your last box-office taking. As soon as those start to sink, your ass is on the hot seat. I've worked too long and too hard to get to where I am to see it all go up in smoke at the first sign of trouble. That's what I do, I make stars and I make money. That's just business. I wouldn't ever hurt her. I just offered her a new contract for god sake.'

You ask about this contract, why it had to be with Peter von Hiltz, too, and not just one or the other. Ramsay's face turns a little redder.

'There are moving parts to that contract that you don't know about, detective,' he says. 'And I'd rather keep them confidential.'

You step forward. He doesn't meet your gaze. You grab him by the lapels of his giant jacket and shake him as best you can, demanding he talk.

'All right,' he says, waving you away. 'All right, fine. If it clears me, so be it. Debra von Hiltz.'

The name doesn't ring any bells. You ask who she is.

'Peter von Hiltz's wife,' says Ramsay. 'Although you can hardly call what they have a marriage. More like an arrangement. He's never been there for her, not a single minute. I can't understand how somebody like von Hiltz can't love and worship the ground that Debra walks on. That's what I do.'

He grows a little glassy-eyed. Looking up at you, he explains.

'Debra and I are deeply in love,' he says. 'We have been for about five years now. We met on one of von Hiltz's pictures for Thundersaga – *Riders of the Old West,* a nasty little western that he brought some prestige and credibility to. Six weeks of shooting in Nevada. I fell in love with her the first time I set eyes on her, honest to god, detective. You dream about things like this happening, especially when you're about to storm a beach in Normandy. But you never think it'll actually happen. The way he treated her on that set, it was appalling. We found each other, just for company at first, but it became clearer and clearer that it was so much more than just companionship. I love her, detective. And she loves me.'

You ask if von Hiltz knows. Ramsay nods.

'He does,' he says flatly. 'Has done for a very long time. They won't divorce, he won't let her. He keeps her hanging on as punishment. He can live with the scandal but he knows I can't, not if I want to stay in my job. Like I said before, I've worked too long and hard to get to where I am. I'm not letting that rat take it all away from me. So we carry on with this pretence, this charade to the rest of the world that she's happily married to von Hiltz and I'm the lonely bachelor betrothed to his job. It's soul-crushing at times, detective, really it is. But we steal as many moments together as we can. Until he twists the knife, like with this new golden handshake deal. He's had me over a barrel but I got back at him, with the clause that it only works with Blanche Aikerman on board. Don't get me wrong, the studio benefits out of that deal, too, of course it does. But that bastard von Hiltz has been aiming for something like this for a long time. And his bitterness has come to fruition.'

Ramsay lets out a huge sigh. He daubs the blood from his forehead and looks sheepishly up at you.

'This is confidential, officer,' he says. 'Only myself, Debra and von Hiltz know about the affair. If it got out then I'd be ruined. I'm begging you, if you can, to keep it all under wraps. I'm sorry for the bribe, I'm just so used to it going that way in this town. Fixers, drug dealers, debt collectors, they all wind up at my door sooner or later. Except for Blanche. She never gave me any trouble, not really. Not until now. I'm exhausted.'

You consider everything that Ramsay has told you. While you're not pleased with how he treats Blanche and the rest of the industry, you believe him that he had nothing to do with the murder. You reach down and uncuff him from the drain pipe.

'Thank you,' he says, getting to his feet. 'I want you to catch whoever did this to Blanche. She was a wonderful girl, talented and beautiful. Money is only money and it keeps the wolves from my door, sure it does. But she was a young woman who was killed for god knows what reason. I saw enough of that pointless slaughter fighting the Nazis. She deserves better than that, as does her mother. She must be devastated, she never left Blanche's side, all day, all night, every day of the year. I can't imagine what's going through *her* mind.'

You ask a question.

- 'Where is von Hiltz now?' (Turn to page 208)

- 'Who was the stranger?' (Turn to page 207)

'It was Walter, the hotel manager,' he says flatly.

He senses you have grown suspicious. Then he laughs gently.

'Don't worry, he's not a killer,' says Ramsay. 'The man is a worm, a snake. He'd do anything for an extra couple of bucks. Sure, he dresses himself up as this stuffed-shirt hotel manager. But he's no better than a common hustler. If there's a chance for him to make a bit of extra dough on the side, he's all over it like a cheap suit. That's fine, it suits me, I don't expect anything less in this town. It's LA, right? That's why I've had him telling me everything that's been going on with Blanche. Who she's been seeing, what she's been eating, who she calls, that kind of thing. Needless to say he was down here telling me she'd been murdered within seconds of your arrival. I keep him sweet by making him think he's part of the gang, that he's on this side of the fence. But I'd drop him in a heartbeat if I could. He's spineless, officer. Trust me, he's no killer.'

- You ask Ramsay where Walter has fled to. Find out on

  page 134

- You ask Ramsay where von Hiltz is now. Find out what Ramsay

  has to say on page 208

'I don't know, I haven't seen him all day,' says the studio executive.

You both head back into the villa, broken glass crunching under your feet from the obliterated patio doors.

'If you find him, you'll find some answers,' he says. 'There are only a few people in this industry as close to Blanche as her mother. One of them was Peter von Hiltz. If he doesn't know who killed her, then he'll have a pretty good idea. But don't trust him, detective. He's a snake in the grass and knows *exactly* how to get what he wants.'

You nod and thank Ramsay for his help in this case. You leave the executive behind in the villa and make your way back into the main lobby of the hotel. Things are getting busy here. Before you plot your next move, the friendly receptionist from earlier waves you down. She has the phone in her hand.

'A call for you, detective,' she says. 'It's your captain from the squad room, he says it's urgent.'

Take the call on page 70.

ACKNOWLEDGEMENTS

The idea of alternative timelines, 'sliding door' moments, multiverses upon multiverses, you name it, has always fascinated me. And getting the chance to write a crime novel with multiple routes, tying me and readers in a knot has been such wonderful fun. Throw into the mix the glitz, glamour and sheer gorgeousness of Golden Age Hollywood and I truly felt like a child in a sweet shop. It's been a total blast and I truly hope you've enjoyed this book as much as I did piecing it together.

There is, as always, a raft of people that I want to thank for getting to this stage. The old adage that it takes a village for a book to come to life has always been a mantra that I adhere to. And 'Tinseltown' is once again a testimony to the hard work and dedication of a small army of brilliant people behind the scenes.

My agent Matthew Cole at Northbank Talent has been an incredibly supportive and enthusiastic champion of this idea. From the very small inklings of writing a puzzle book set in 1950s Hollywood to endlessly praising the work to the hilt, I am hugely grateful for his patience, professionalism and advice.

The HarperNorth team has, as always, been their wonderful selves. Ben McConnell has my complete adoration – not just for being a wonderful editor, but for putting up with the confusing, mind-boggling and downright chaotic nature of the first draft of a book like this. His boundless charm and steady hand have been integral in bringing my vision to life. And for that I will be eternally in his debt. The same goes for Megan Jones, who has remained one of the constants throughout my writing career. Knowing that she has been a part of this project has been the steady rock that makes a jittery, email-at-all-hours-happy writer like me take solace and confidence that everything will be alright in the end.

A number of author friends also need to be thanked for their help. The brilliant Antony Johnston has been at the end of a phone and laptop, always ready to deliver his own indomitable brand of advice and good sense. Steven Kedie and Chris McDonald, for being such superb supporters of me, my work and my half-baked ideas. Hannah Mary McKinnon, who showed such enthusiasm for the idea from the off. And last, but by no means least, Nasheema Lennon for being a total star and celebrating the writing journey at every twist and turn.

Finally, I want to thank my family, as I always do. Without their kindness and love, I'm unable to do horrible fictional things to lovely people and eventually catch the baddies. Their energy is infectious. No amount of words will ever be enough to express my thanks.

Harper North

would like to thank the following staff and contributors for their involvement in making this book a reality:

Fionnuala Barrett
Peter Borcsok
Katie Buckley
Sarah Burke
Nathan Burton
Alan Cracknell
Jonathan de Peyer
Anna Derkacz
Tom Dunstan
Kate Elton
Sarah Emsley
Simon Gerratt
Monica Green
Natassa Hadjinicolaou
Guy Holland
Megan Jones
Jean-Marie Kelly
Taslima Khatun

Rachel McCarron
Ben McConnell
Petra Moll
Alice Murphy-Pyle
Adam Murray
Genevieve Pegg
Amanda Percival
Natasha Photiou
Florence Shepherd
Colleen Simpson
Eleanor Slater
Hilary Stein
Emma Sullivan
Emily Thomas
Katrina Troy
Daisy Watt
Emma Hatlen

For more unmissable reads,
sign up to the HarperNorth newsletter at
www.harpernorth.co.uk

or find us on Twitter at
@HarperNorthUK

**Harper
North**